Nordic Shadows: The Architect

Daniel Fankhauser

Contents

Chapter 1: Blood on the Rocks

The sound of crashing waves echoed against the rocky coastline of Smögen, the first light of dawn casting a pale orange glow over the horizon. Sofia Andersson jogged along the narrow cliff path, her breath fogging in the chilly morning air. She had always loved these early runs, a time when the town was still asleep, the sea whispering secrets only she could hear.

But today was different.

As she rounded a bend, her eyes caught something unusual—a flash of red amidst the grey stones below. At first, she thought it was driftwood or seaweed washed ashore, but as she got closer, her breath hitched. A human figure lay sprawled on the rocks, blood pooling around the jagged edges. The man's face was turned away, but the unnatural angle of his limbs left no doubt. He was dead.

Her scream cut through the quiet morning.

Detective Erik Sandström arrived at the scene thirty minutes later, his expression as grim as the weather. He stepped carefully across the slick rocks, his boots crunching on frost-coated seaweed. Lars Holm, his younger partner, was already there, his jaw tight as he gestured toward the body.

"Male, mid-forties," Lars said, his voice clipped. "Likely fell—or was pushed. But look at this."

He pointed to the victim's chest, where a deep stab wound was visible through the torn fabric of his jacket.

Erik crouched beside the body, his sharp blue eyes narrowing. The faint scent of salt and iron mingled in the air. "This wasn't an accident," he murmured. "It's murder."

Erik straightened, his coat whipping in the biting wind as he took in the scene. The jagged rocks were stained crimson where the body had fallen, and tiny shards of glass glimmered near the victim's outstretched hand. He gestured toward Lars.

"Photographs. Document everything," Erik ordered. "And cordon off the area—this place will be crawling with reporters by midday."

Lars nodded, pulling out his camera with practiced efficiency. Despite his relative inexperience in homicide cases, Lars had a methodical precision Erik appreciated—though the younger man's occasional eagerness to jump to conclusions often grated on him.

As Lars snapped pictures, a new figure approached from the cliff path above. Dr. Ingrid Westin, Smögen's forensic specialist, climbed down carefully, her bag slung over her shoulder.

"Another bad morning for a walk," she said, her voice cool but laced with exhaustion. She had been called to the last big case in Smögen, a drowning incident that turned out to be murder—a memory that still lingered in the tightness of her jaw.

Erik gave a brief nod. "Looks like you'll have your hands full again."

Ingrid crouched beside the body, snapping on gloves with a practiced motion. Her gaze scanned the stab wound, the bruising around the arms, and the shallow cuts on the victim's hands. "Defensive wounds," she said softly. "He fought back."

"And lost," Lars added grimly.

"Check his pockets," Erik said, stepping back to give Ingrid space. "ID, anything that can give us a lead."

Ingrid carefully turned the body, exposing a wallet tucked into the man's inner coat pocket. She handed it to Erik, who opened it with a frown.

"Karl Nyström," he read aloud. "Address matches one of the larger homes by the marina." He glanced at Lars. "Get someone to notify the family. And get ready for a lot of questions—they'll want to know why their loved one was stabbed to death."

Lars exhaled slowly, already dreading the task. "I'll handle it."

The Nyström-Villa

The Nyström villa loomed large at the edge of the marina, its whitewashed walls stark against the morning's dull grey sky. Lars stood at the iron gate, hesitating for a moment before pressing the doorbell. The chime echoed through the house, a hollow sound that seemed to mock him.

Annika Nyström appeared moments later, her figure silhouetted in the doorway. She was tall and elegant, her dark hair pulled into a tight bun. Her sharp cheekbones and piercing blue eyes gave her a striking appearance, but there was a coldness to her that immediately unsettled Lars.

"Yes?" she said, her voice steady but guarded.

Lars cleared his throat. "Mrs. Nyström, I'm Lars Holm from the Smögen police. May I come in?"

Annika's expression flickered for a moment, something between curiosity and dread crossing her face. She stepped aside, gesturing for him to enter.

The interior of the house was pristine, the kind of perfection that suggested more control than comfort. A faint scent of lavender hung in the air, and everything—from the polished floors to the carefully arranged bookshelves—seemed meticulously curated.

"I'm afraid I have some difficult news," Lars began, his voice as gentle as he could make it. "Your husband, Karl, was found dead this morning."

Annika stared at him, her face frozen in shock. For a moment, she said nothing, her hands tightening on the back of a chair. Then, as if on cue, she sank into the seat, her gaze fixed on the floor.

"How?" she whispered finally, her voice barely audible.

"We believe he was murdered," Lars said, choosing his words carefully. "The investigation is ongoing, but I assure you we'll do everything we can to find out who did this."

Annika's hands trembled slightly, but her expression remained composed. "Murdered," she repeated, almost to herself. "Who would do such a thing?"

"That's what we're here to find out," Lars replied. "Did your husband mention any threats recently? Anyone he was worried about?"

She shook her head slowly, her lips pressed into a thin line. "Karl had his disagreements—mostly business matters—but nothing that would..." Her voice trailed off, and she looked away, as though she were afraid to finish the thought.

Lars watched her closely, noting the subtle tension in her posture. He had seen grief take many forms over the years, but something about Annika's reaction didn't sit right with him.

"We'll need to ask you a few more questions later," he said, rising to leave. "For now, I'd suggest you stay here. If you think of anything—anything at all—please call us."

Annika nodded, her gaze distant. As Lars stepped outside, he couldn't shake the feeling that she was hiding something.

Back at the station, Detective Erik Sandström leaned over the case board, tacking up a photograph of Karl Nyström's body. The image was stark, the lifeless eyes and blood-soaked rocks demanding answers. Beside it, he pinned a map of the coastline, marking the exact spot where the body had been found.

The room smelled faintly of stale coffee and damp paper, a testament to long hours and few breaks. Lars entered with a sigh, shrugging off his jacket and throwing it over the back of his chair.

"How did it go with Annika?" Erik asked without looking up.

"She took it... strangely," Lars replied, sinking into his seat. "No tears. She seemed shocked, but not in the way you'd expect. I don't know, something about her felt off."

Erik glanced at him. "Grief doesn't follow a script. Some people shut down completely."

"Or they're hiding something," Lars muttered, staring at the board.

Before Erik could respond, Ingrid Westin stepped into the room, her medical bag slung over one shoulder and a file in her hand. Her crisp movements and calm demeanor gave her an air of authority that Erik had come to rely on.

"I've finished the preliminary autopsy," she said, placing the file on the desk. "Karl Nyström sustained a single stab wound to the chest, likely from a blade about six inches long. The angle suggests a left-handed assailant."

Lars raised an eyebrow. "Anything else?"

Ingrid nodded, flipping through the report. "There are defensive wounds on his hands and forearms—he definitely fought back. But there's something else." She hesitated, her brow furrowing. "I found traces of a toxin in his bloodstream. It's not something you'd come across every day. I've sent it off for further analysis, but it's likely what incapacitated him before the fatal wound."

"A toxin?" Erik repeated, straightening. "Do you think it was deliberate, or could it have been accidental?"

"Hard to say without more information," Ingrid replied. "But it doesn't feel accidental. Whoever did this knew what they were doing."

Erik's jaw tightened. A murder weapon, a possible poisoning, and now the murky motives of a grieving widow—it was beginning to feel like an intricate puzzle with too many missing pieces.

"Lars, dig deeper into Karl's business dealings," Erik said. "If he was targeted, someone had a reason. And Ingrid, let me know the moment the toxin report comes back. We're not ruling anything out."

Lars nodded, already pulling up files on his laptop, while Ingrid left the room with a curt nod. Erik remained by the case board, his eyes narrowing as he studied the photographs.

The pieces didn't fit yet, but they would.

The Autopsy Report

The hum of the police station grew quieter as the day wore on, the weight of the investigation settling heavily over the small team. Erik sat at his desk, reviewing the details Ingrid had provided in the autopsy report. The mention of the toxin lingered in his mind. It was rare, deliberate, and hinted at a methodical killer.

Across the room, Lars was deep in conversation on the phone. Erik listened in as his partner scribbled notes furiously. "Got it," Lars said, hanging up and turning to Erik. "Karl's business wasn't as clean as it looked. He was involved in some shady deals with a man named Jonas Söderberg—a name that's been flagged before in illegal fishing rings."

"Illegal fishing?" Erik asked, his brow furrowing.

"Smuggling, actually," Lars replied. "Expensive seafood shipped off the books to buyers overseas. There's a lot of money in it, and it's dangerous. Söderberg's been on our radar, but we've never had enough to pin him down."

Erik leaned back, his mind racing. If Karl was tangled up with Söderberg, it opened a whole new avenue of suspects—and motives.

"Do we know if Karl and Söderberg had any recent disputes?" Erik asked.

"Not yet," Lars admitted. "But I've reached out to a couple of informants. If there's dirt, we'll find it."

Before Erik could respond, his desk phone buzzed. He answered it, his expression tightening as he listened.

"We've got another problem," Erik said, hanging up. "The Nyström villa's been vandalized. Someone smashed in the windows and spray-painted the walls. Annika's terrified."

"Do you think it's connected to the murder?" Lars asked.

"It has to be," Erik replied. "Someone's trying to send a message—or cover their tracks. Let's head over."

The two detectives grabbed their coats and headed for the car. The drive to the Nyström villa was tense, neither man speaking as they processed the latest development.

When they arrived, Annika was pacing in the front yard, her face pale and drawn. Red graffiti scrawled across the villa's white walls read: "You deserved this."

Erik approached her carefully. "Mrs. Nyström, did you see who did this?"

She shook her head, her voice trembling. "I heard the glass shatter, but by the time I got outside, they were gone."

"Did Karl ever mention anyone who might have wanted to threaten him—or you?"

Annika hesitated, her arms crossed tightly. "I don't know," she said finally. "He kept a lot to himself. There were people he argued with, but nothing like this. It's like he had a double life I didn't know about."

Erik exchanged a look with Lars. A double life. It explained a lot—and it made things infinitely more complicated.

"We'll post an officer outside tonight," Erik said, his voice firm. "And we'll need access to any of Karl's personal records—emails, phone calls, anything you can think of."

Annika nodded, though her expression was distant. Erik studied her carefully, the pieces of the puzzle beginning to shift into focus.

As the detectives returned to their car, Lars broke the silence. "If this was a message, someone's getting nervous. That means we're getting closer."

"Let's hope they don't get too desperate before we figure out who it is," Erik replied, starting the engine.

The case was heating up, but the danger was far from over.

Chapter 2: The Silent Witness

The harbor bustled with its usual morning activity—fishermen unloading their early catches, gulls squawking as they dove for scraps, and the faint hum of boats leaving the docks. Yet beneath the surface, the tension in Smögen was palpable. The murder of Karl Nyström had spread like wildfire through the close-knit town, whispers and rumors swirling in every corner.

Erik stood near the docks, his sharp eyes scanning the marina. He had spent the morning interviewing locals, hoping someone had seen or heard something unusual the night Karl was killed. So far, all he had gotten were dead ends and suspiciously vague answers.

Lars approached, his expression grim. “No one wants to talk,” he said, shoving his hands into his jacket pockets. “It’s like they’re afraid of something—or someone.”

“They probably are,” Erik replied, his voice low. “A murder like this doesn’t happen in isolation. There’s a reason Karl was killed, and I doubt it was random.”

Before Lars could respond, an elderly fisherman approached, his weathered face lined with years of sun and salt. Olle Lindqvist was one of the harbor’s most respected figures, known for his sharp memory and sharper tongue.

“I heard you’ve been asking questions,” Olle said, his gaze fixed on Erik.

“That’s right,” Erik replied, turning to face him. “Did you see or hear anything unusual the night Karl Nyström was killed?”

Olle hesitated, his weathered hands gripping the brim of his cap. “I didn’t see much,” he began, his voice cautious. “But I heard a commotion down by Pier 7 late that night. Voices. Angry ones.”

“Did you recognize anyone?” Lars asked, stepping closer.

The old man shook his head. “It was dark. And I wasn’t about to stick my nose where it didn’t belong. But I did see a boat leaving the harbor not long after. Small, with no lights. Headed west.”

Erik exchanged a glance with Lars. Pier 7 was one of the quieter spots in the marina, a place where people went to avoid attention. If Karl had been there the night of his death, it could explain the lack of witnesses.

“Can you describe the boat?” Erik asked.

Olle shrugged. “Just a shadow in the water. But it looked familiar—like it belonged to someone local.”

The detective nodded, filing the information away. A boat leaving the harbor in the dead of night might be their first solid lead.

“Thank you, Olle,” Erik said. “If you remember anything else, no matter how small, let us know.”

Olle nodded, tipping his cap before turning to leave.

As he disappeared into the crowd, Lars sighed. “A shadow in the water. Not much to go on.”

“It’s more than we had an hour ago,” Erik replied. “Let’s see if anyone else at the marina knows about that boat. Someone must have seen it.”

The marina office was a modest structure perched on the edge of the harbor, its weathered wood exterior speaking to years of salt-laden winds and relentless sea air. Erik and Lars stepped inside, the faint smell of diesel and damp paper filling the small room. Behind the counter sat Greta Andersson, the harbor manager, her sharp eyes and no-nonsense demeanor well-known among the fishermen.

“Detectives,” Greta greeted them curtly, barely looking up from her paperwork. “What brings you here this morning?”

“We’re looking into the murder of Karl Nyström,” Erik said. “We’ve been told a boat left the harbor late the night he was killed. Small, no lights. Headed west. Any chance you know anything about it?”

Greta leaned back in her chair, folding her arms. “A boat leaving without lights? That’s against regulations.”

“Which makes it all the more interesting,” Lars added, his tone dry.

Greta sighed, her fingers drumming against the desk. “I didn’t see anything myself, but...” She trailed off, her eyes narrowing in thought. “There’s a security camera near Pier 7. It’s not the best quality, but it might’ve caught something.”

“That’s exactly what we need,” Erik said.

Greta pushed herself up from her chair and motioned for them to follow. They entered a cramped back room filled with monitors, most showing live feeds of the harbor. She rewound the footage from the night of the murder, the grainy black-and-white images flickering on the screen.

“There,” she said, pointing. The timestamp showed 11:43 p.m. A small boat drifted into view, its outline barely visible in the dim light. No navigation lights were on, and the boat’s movements were slow and deliberate.

"Can you zoom in?" Lars asked.

Greta shook her head. "That's as clear as it gets. I told you, the camera's old. We've been meaning to replace it."

Erik studied the screen, his eyes narrowing. "That boat's heading west, just like Olle said. Do you recognize it?"

Greta squinted at the screen. "Hard to say. It could be half the boats in this harbor. But the size... it looks a lot like Björn Lindholm's skiff. He keeps it docked over by Pier 9."

"Björn Lindholm," Lars repeated, scribbling the name into his notebook. "What do you know about him?"

Greta shrugged. "Quiet guy. Keeps to himself. He's been here for years, but no one really knows much about him. His boat's been in the shop a few times, but nothing unusual."

"Thanks, Greta," Erik said. "We'll take it from here."

Back outside, Lars glanced at Erik. "Do you think this Björn is our guy?"

"I think he's someone we need to talk to," Erik replied. "Let's head to Pier 9."

The walk to Pier 9 was short but tense, the cold wind biting at their faces. When they reached the dock, Björn's skiff was exactly where Greta had said it would be. The small boat rocked gently in the water, its paint peeling and its name—Sjöfågel—faded but legible.

"Looks like it hasn't moved in days," Lars observed, crouching to inspect the mooring lines.

"Or someone was careful enough to cover their tracks," Erik muttered.

They knocked on Björn Lindholm's door, a modest shack at the end of the pier. No answer. Erik knocked again, harder this time. Still nothing.

"Do you think he skipped town?" Lars asked.

"Maybe," Erik said, his jaw tightening. "Or maybe he's hiding. Either way, we need to find him."

Erik and Lars didn't waste time. If Björn Lindholm wasn't at his shack, they needed to track him down quickly. The longer he stayed missing, the more suspicious his absence became. Erik glanced at the peeling paint of the door and the cracked window beside it. It didn't look like someone had prepared for a hasty getaway, but still, Björn's unexplained absence gnawed at his instincts.

"Let's check with some of the other dock workers," Erik said. "If he's not here, someone must know where he's gone."

They walked down the pier, where a group of fishermen were mending nets. Most of them cast wary glances at the detectives, clearly aware of the murder investigation. Erik's presence alone was enough to unsettle the typically tight-lipped harbor workers.

"Excuse me," Erik said, addressing a man with a wiry frame and a cigarette dangling from his lips. "We're looking for Björn Lindholm. Have you seen him recently?"

The man paused, his gaze flickering toward the shack before returning to Erik. "Not since yesterday afternoon," he said cautiously. "He was down here fixing his nets. Left around sunset, didn't say where he was going."

"Did he seem unusual in any way?" Lars asked.

The man shrugged. "Björn's always quiet. Keeps to himself. But now that you mention it... he looked nervous. Kept glancing around like someone was watching him."

"Do you know if he's involved in anything—off the books?" Erik pressed, watching the man's reaction closely.

The fisherman hesitated, taking a long drag on his cigarette before exhaling slowly. "If he is, he doesn't talk about it. But he's been spending more time out on the water lately. Night trips, mostly."

"Night trips," Erik repeated. "Where does he go?"

"Couldn't say," the man replied. "He doesn't invite company."

The conversation ended with the same cryptic undertones as it began. Erik thanked the man before heading back toward the shack with Lars.

"We're missing something," Lars said as they reached the dock. "Björn's not the kind of guy to run unless he has a reason. If he knows something about Karl, it might've scared him off."

"Or he's more involved than we realize," Erik replied, his voice low. He stepped closer to the boat, examining its exterior. The peeling paint and weathered surface made it look like a forgotten relic of the harbor, but Erik noticed something strange: the inside of the hull was damp, as though it had been used recently.

"He took this boat out," Erik muttered. "Not long ago, either."

Before Lars could respond, Erik's phone buzzed. He answered it, his expression darkening as he listened.

"Understood," he said before hanging up. He turned to Lars, his tone sharp. "Ingrid just called. They've identified the toxin in Karl's blood. It's from a venom extracted from cone snails. Highly potent, highly rare."

Lars frowned. "Cone snail venom? Who even knows how to get their hands on something like that?"

"Someone with very specific knowledge," Erik said. "And very specific intentions." He looked back at Björn's skiff. "We need to bring this boat in for a full search. There's something here—we just haven't found it yet."

The Sjöfågel

The sun dipped lower in the sky as Erik and Lars waited for the forensics team to arrive at the marina. The Sjöfågel sat quietly at Pier 9, its peeling paint and worn ropes belying the possible secrets it held. Erik paced the dock, his sharp eyes scanning the water and nearby boats, searching for anything that might connect Björn Lindholm to Karl Nyström's death.

When the forensics van finally pulled up, Ingrid Westin stepped out, carrying her ever-present case of tools. Her movements were precise as she made her way toward the boat, her expression calm but focused.

"Cone snail venom," she said by way of greeting, handing Erik a sealed vial containing a sample. "It's nearly impossible to get your hands on this unless you know exactly where to look—and exactly what you're doing. If this is linked to Björn, we need to understand how."

"We're hoping the boat will tell us something," Erik replied. "Have at it."

Ingrid climbed aboard the Sjöfågel, her gloved hands methodically opening compartments and inspecting every crevice. Lars stood by, watching her work while Erik returned to pacing. The tension in the air was palpable, each minute feeling heavier than the last.

"Erik," Ingrid called out after several minutes. "I've found something."

Erik and Lars quickly joined her on the boat. She held up a small metal case, its latches rusted but intact. "It was wedged under one of the floorboards," she said.

Erik knelt down as Ingrid opened the case. Inside was a collection of syringes, a few small glass vials, and a notebook. The labels on the vials were handwritten in Swedish, each one identifying a different toxin.

"Definitely not your average fishing supplies," Lars muttered.

Ingrid frowned, carefully examining the vials. "This one," she said, holding up a vial labeled **'Cone Toxin—Batch 12'**, "matches the venom found in Karl's system."

Erik flipped open the notebook, scanning the entries. The handwriting was messy, but it detailed experiments, dosages, and effects—notes that clearly required a high level of knowledge about toxins and their uses.

"This is calculated," Erik said, his voice hard. "Whoever wrote this knows exactly what they're doing. This isn't just amateur experimentation."

"Björn Lindholm doesn't strike me as a biochemist," Lars said. "But maybe he's working for someone who is."

"Or he's deeper in this than we thought," Erik countered. "Either way, we need to find him now."

As they stepped off the boat, Erik's phone buzzed. He answered, listening intently for a moment before his jaw tightened.

"That was dispatch," he said, slipping the phone into his pocket. "Björn Lindholm's been spotted. He rented a room at a guesthouse just outside of town. Let's move."

The guesthouse was a small, quaint building surrounded by thick pines, its whitewashed exterior nearly blending into the snowy landscape. Erik and Lars approached cautiously, their senses heightened. The guesthouse manager, a timid woman in her sixties, met them at the door.

"Room 4," she whispered, pointing to the staircase. "He's been quiet since he checked in last night."

Erik nodded and motioned for Lars to follow. The wooden stairs creaked under their weight as they climbed to the second floor. Outside Room 4, Erik paused, his hand hovering over the doorknob. He nodded at Lars, who drew his weapon, and then Erik knocked.

“Björn Lindholm,” Erik called out. “This is the police. We need to talk.”

Silence.

Erik knocked again, harder this time. “Björn, we know you’re in there. Open the door.”

A faint sound came from inside—movement, hurried and frantic. Erik exchanged a quick glance with Lars before trying the doorknob. It was locked.

“We’re going in,” Erik said, stepping back to kick the door open.

The door slammed against the wall as they entered, weapons drawn. The room was sparsely furnished, but the bed was unmade, and a duffel bag sat open on the floor. In the far corner, Björn Lindholm stood, his hands raised, his face pale and drawn.

“Don’t shoot!” he stammered. “I didn’t do anything!”

“Then you’ve got nothing to worry about,” Erik said coldly. “We’re taking you in for questioning.”

The Toxin

The interrogation room was as stark as ever, its white walls devoid of any comfort. Björn Lindholm sat hunched over in the metal chair, his hands clasped together, his eyes darting nervously between Erik and Lars. The room was suffocatingly quiet, save for the faint hum of the overhead lights.

“Björn,” Erik began, his voice calm but firm, “you’re not under arrest—yet. But you need to be honest with us. Why did you run?”

Björn shifted in his seat, his knuckles white as he gripped his hands tighter. “I didn’t run,” he said, his voice barely above a whisper. “I just... needed time to think.”

“To think about what?” Lars pressed, leaning forward.

Björn hesitated, his eyes fixed on the table. “I didn’t kill him,” he said finally. “I swear, I didn’t kill Karl Nyström.”

“We didn’t say you did,” Erik replied, his tone measured. “But you were seen leaving the harbor the night of the murder. Your boat matches the description of the one spotted heading west. And we found cone snail venom on your boat—the same toxin used on Karl. Care to explain that?”

Björn’s head shot up, his face pale. “That wasn’t mine!” he protested. “I don’t even know what that stuff is. Someone must’ve put it there.”

“Who?” Lars demanded. “You expect us to believe someone snuck onto your boat, planted the venom, and then disappeared?”

“I don’t know!” Björn’s voice cracked. “I don’t know who it was, but it wasn’t me!”

Erik exchanged a glance with Lars before leaning forward, his gaze steady. “Björn, you’re in deep trouble. If you don’t start telling us the truth, things will only get worse for you. Let’s start simple. Why were you out on the water that night?”

Björn swallowed hard, his Adam's apple bobbing. "I... I was supposed to meet someone," he admitted.

"Who?" Erik pressed.

Björn's hands trembled as he wiped them on his pants. "Jonas Söderberg," he said finally. "He told me to meet him near the cliffs west of the harbor. Said he had a job for me."

"And what kind of job would that be?" Lars asked, his tone sharp.

"I didn't ask," Björn muttered. "I just needed the money. Times have been tough, and Jonas pays well. But when I got there, he wasn't alone. Karl was with him."

Erik's jaw tightened. "What happened next?"

Björn shook his head, his eyes glassy. "They were arguing. Shouting. I stayed on the boat—I didn't want to get involved. Then I saw... I saw Jonas push Karl."

"Push him where?" Lars demanded.

"Off the rocks," Björn whispered. "Karl fell. I didn't know what to do, so I left."

Erik leaned back in his chair, his mind racing. Jonas Söderberg—a name that kept surfacing but remained elusive. If Björn's story was true, Jonas was directly involved in Karl's death.

"Why didn't you come forward?" Erik asked.

Björn's gaze dropped to the table. "Because Jonas is dangerous," he said. "And if he finds out I talked to you, I'm as good as dead."

Lars leaned back, running a hand through his hair. "This Jonas just keeps getting more interesting."

Erik stood, his hands resting on the table. "Björn, you're not going anywhere. We'll verify your story, but if you're lying..." He let the sentence hang in the air before heading for the door.

As he and Lars left the room, Ingrid was waiting for them in the hallway.

“What’s your take?” she asked.

“He’s scared,” Erik replied. “But there’s a kernel of truth in there. If Jonas Söderberg was at the scene, we need to find him—and fast.”

Chapter 3: The Vanishing Alibi

The search for Jonas Söderberg began at sunrise, the golden light of dawn casting long shadows across Smögen's narrow streets and rugged cliffs. Erik and Lars had spent the night compiling everything they knew about Jonas—a man with a reputation for skirting the law but who always managed to avoid getting caught. Now, the task was simple but daunting: track him down before he vanished for good.

The first stop was Söderberg's known address, a modest cabin tucked away near the edge of town, surrounded by tall pines that swayed in the morning breeze. Erik parked the car, and the two detectives approached cautiously, their senses on high alert. The cabin's windows were dark, its wooden walls weathered and worn.

"Do you think he's here?" Lars asked, his voice low.

Erik shook his head. "No car in the driveway, no signs of life. But let's check."

They knocked on the door, the sound echoing into the quiet woods. No answer. Erik tried again, harder this time, but the cabin remained silent. Lars moved to peer through one of the windows, shielding his eyes from the glare of the morning sun.

"Looks empty," Lars said. "No movement inside. Just... a mess. Papers everywhere."

Erik tried the door handle—it was locked. Pulling a small set of tools from his pocket, he worked quickly, the lock clicking open within seconds. "Let's take a look."

The inside of the cabin was chaotic, the air stale. Papers were strewn across the floor, a chair lay overturned, and an empty coffee cup sat on the table, the dregs dried at the bottom. It didn't look like someone had left in a hurry, but rather as though they had been living in a constant state of disarray.

Erik moved to the desk, where a stack of documents caught his eye. He sifted through them, noting financial records, receipts, and scribbled notes. Lars, meanwhile, focused on the bookshelves, pulling out binders and flipping through their contents.

"Here," Erik said, holding up a torn envelope with the name **Karl Nyström** scrawled across it. "Looks like correspondence. The handwriting matches the notebook we found on Björn's boat."

Lars walked over to examine the envelope. "So, they were definitely in contact. But what does this mean?"

"Means Jonas was lying low, but he wasn't hiding his connections to Karl," Erik replied. He flipped open the envelope, pulling out a single piece of paper. The message was short and chilling: **"Meet me tonight at the cliffs. We need to settle this—once and for all."**

"Looks like Karl wasn't the only one with secrets," Lars said grimly.

Before Erik could respond, his phone buzzed. He answered quickly, his expression darkening as he listened.

"Understood," he said before hanging up. He turned to Lars, his jaw tight. "That was Ingrid. Björn's story checks out—cone snail venom was used on Karl, and the handwriting on this letter matches the notebook. But there's more: a second set of prints were found on the vials in Björn's boat. They're not his."

"So, Jonas wasn't just involved," Lars said. "He was pulling the strings."

"Let's hope we're not too late to prove it," Erik replied. "We need to track him down before he disappears."

The clues they had gathered painted a grim picture, but Erik knew that assumptions could be dangerous. As he and Lars left

Söderberg's cabin, the bitter cold seemed sharper than before, the weight of the case pressing down harder with each step.

Back at the station, the case board was quickly filling with connections—pictures of Karl Nyström, the venom vial from Björn's boat, and now Jonas Söderberg's cryptic note. Lars added the envelope to the board while Erik stared at the tangled web of evidence.

"It doesn't add up," Erik muttered, his fingers tracing the line between Karl's photo and Jonas' name. "If Jonas planned to meet Karl, why bring venom? Why not just confront him? This feels... orchestrated."

"Maybe Jonas wasn't the one pulling the strings," Lars suggested. "What if he's just another pawn in all this?"

Erik glanced at his partner, considering the possibility. "Then we need to find the one holding the strings."

Their discussion was interrupted by a knock at the door. Ingrid entered, a file in hand and a look of urgency in her eyes.

"I ran a deeper analysis on the venom," she said, placing the file on the desk. "It's not just cone snail venom—it's been altered. Whoever created this knew what they were doing. It's more concentrated, more lethal."

"And you're certain it wasn't Björn?" Erik asked.

Ingrid nodded. "Positive. He doesn't have the skill or the resources. But the handwriting on the vials—there's a second sample. It matches a known profile from our database. A name tied to biochemistry smuggling."

"Who?" Lars asked.

Ingrid hesitated before answering. "Axel Bergström. He's an independent contractor—worked for pharmaceutical companies before he was fired for unethical experiments. He's been under the radar for years, but his name surfaces in illegal trade now and then."

Erik leaned forward, the pieces clicking into place. "If Axel is involved, he could be the one who supplied the venom. And if Jonas was working with him, it means Karl wasn't their first victim."

"Or their last," Ingrid added grimly.

Erik pushed back from the desk, grabbing his coat. "We need to bring Jonas in now. He's our only lead to Axel."

The next stop was a bar near the docks, a dimly lit watering hole frequented by fishermen and loners who knew the sea better than their neighbors. Jonas Söderberg was said to drink there often, and Erik hoped the whispers of his presence would lead them closer.

The smell of salt and stale beer hit them as they entered. The room was sparsely populated—groups of men huddled around tables, their faces shadowed in the dim light. Erik approached the bartender, a burly man cleaning a glass with a dishrag that looked older than Erik himself.

"We're looking for Jonas Söderberg," Erik said, sliding his badge across the counter.

The bartender glanced at the badge, then at Erik, his expression unreadable. "Haven't seen him."

Lars leaned in. "This isn't the time for games. We know he comes here."

The bartender hesitated before nodding toward a back booth. "He was here earlier. Didn't stay long. Looked like he was in a hurry."

Erik's eyes followed the gesture, landing on an empty booth in the shadows. A crumpled napkin lay on the table, next to an empty glass. Erik moved quickly, picking up the napkin. Scrawled on it in the same messy handwriting as the note to Karl was another short message:

"Pier 12. Midnight."

"He's making his move," Erik said, showing Lars the napkin. "We've got a location."

"Do you think he knows we're onto him?" Lars asked.

"I think he's desperate," Erik replied. "Desperate people make mistakes. Let's make sure we're there when he does."

Pier 12

Pier 12 was desolate when Erik and Lars arrived, the moon casting a pale glow over the water. The creaking of the boats and the occasional slap of waves against the pier were the only sounds in the still night. A heavy fog rolled in from the sea, blanketing the area in an eerie haze. Erik tightened his grip on his flashlight, scanning the shadows.

"This feels like a setup," Lars muttered, his hand resting on his holstered weapon.

"It probably is," Erik replied. "But if Jonas is here, we can't let him slip away again."

The detectives moved cautiously down the pier, their boots echoing against the worn wooden planks. Erik stopped suddenly, raising a hand. A faint outline of a figure emerged at the end of the pier, motionless and shrouded in fog.

"Jonas Söderberg?" Erik called out, his voice steady.

The figure didn't respond, but it shifted slightly, as if weighing its options.

"Jonas, we need to talk," Erik continued. "If you cooperate, we can help you. But if you run, it only gets worse for you."

For a moment, the figure didn't move. Then, as if jolted into action, it turned and bolted toward a small boat moored at the edge of the pier.

"Stop!" Lars shouted, sprinting after him. Erik followed close behind, the adrenaline surging through his veins as Jonas leapt onto the boat, fumbling to untie the mooring lines.

Erik reached the edge of the pier just as Jonas pushed the boat away. Without hesitation, Erik jumped onto the deck, landing hard and knocking Jonas off balance.

The two men grappled in the confined space, the boat rocking violently under their weight. Jonas swung wildly, catching Erik's arm, but Erik managed to twist free and pin him against the side of the boat.

"Enough!" Erik barked, breathing heavily. "It's over, Jonas."

Jonas struggled briefly before slumping in defeat. Lars appeared moments later, jumping aboard and snapping handcuffs onto Jonas' wrists.

"We could've done this the easy way," Lars muttered, dragging Jonas to his feet.

"You don't understand," Jonas gasped. "If you arrest me, he'll kill me. Axel will kill me!"

Erik's gaze sharpened. "Axel Bergström? Where is he?"

Jonas shook his head frantically. "I don't know! He doesn't tell me where he goes. I just do what he says—he supplies the venom, and I... I handle the rest."

"Handle the rest?" Erik repeated, his voice ice-cold. "Like Karl Nyström?"

Jonas froze, his eyes wide with fear. "It wasn't supposed to happen like that. Axel wanted me to scare Karl, not kill him. But things got out of control."

Lars tightened his grip on Jonas' arm. "So you admit you were there?"

"Yes!" Jonas shouted. "I was there, but I didn't mean to—"

"Save it," Erik snapped, cutting him off. "You're coming with us, and you're going to tell us everything about Axel—where he operates, who he works with, and what else you're involved in."

Jonas sagged in Lars' grip, the fight drained out of him. "You don't understand," he whispered. "Axel doesn't leave loose ends. If he knows I've talked to you, I'm dead."

"That's not your concern anymore," Erik said firmly. "Your only chance is to work with us. Let's go."

The drive back to the station was tense. Jonas sat in the back seat, his hands cuffed in front of him, his head bowed as if trying to disappear into the shadows. Erik and Lars exchanged occasional glances, but neither spoke. The weight of Jonas' revelations hung heavy in the air.

When they arrived at the station, Erik led Jonas to the interrogation room, gesturing for Lars to join him. Jonas hesitated as he entered, his eyes darting around the stark space. The click of the cuffs being secured to the table seemed to echo louder than usual.

"Jonas," Erik began as he sat across from him, "you need to tell us everything you know about Axel Bergström. If you hold anything back, you're putting yourself in more danger."

Jonas shifted in his seat, his shoulders hunched. "You don't get it," he whispered. "Axel's not just some guy you can track down. He's smart—always two steps ahead. And he's ruthless. He doesn't care who gets hurt, as long as he gets what he wants."

"What does he want?" Lars asked, leaning against the wall, his arms crossed.

Jonas exhaled shakily. "Money, power, control. He doesn't just deal in venom. He's got connections in illegal pharma, smuggling, even arms deals. He's building something big, but I don't know what. I'm just... small-time to him."

"You were more than small-time when Karl Nyström ended up dead," Erik said, his tone cold. "What happened that night?"

Jonas rubbed his face with his hands, his cuffs clinking against the table. "Karl was getting in the way. Axel needed him to stay quiet, to back off some land deal they were both involved in. I don't know the details, but Axel thought threatening him would work. He sent me to meet Karl and scare him. That's all I was supposed to do."

"And instead, Karl ended up dead," Erik pressed.

"It wasn't me!" Jonas shouted, his voice breaking. "I swear, I didn't kill him. We argued, yeah, and things got heated. But before I could do anything, Axel showed up. He wasn't supposed to be there."

"Axel was there?" Lars interjected, stepping closer.

Jonas nodded frantically. "He must've followed me or something. I don't know. But when he showed up, Karl freaked out. They started yelling at each other, and the next thing I know, Axel... he pushed Karl."

"Off the cliffs?" Erik asked, his tone sharp.

Jonas hesitated, then nodded. "Yes. Karl lost his balance and went over. I didn't even have time to react."

"Then what?" Lars demanded.

"I panicked," Jonas admitted. "Axel told me to leave, said he'd clean it up. I didn't ask questions—I just got out of there."

Erik sat back, his mind racing. If Jonas was telling the truth, Axel wasn't just orchestrating the operation—he was directly responsible for Karl's death. But Jonas' fear of Axel wasn't just about retaliation. It was about survival.

"Where is Axel now?" Erik asked, his voice steady.

"I don't know," Jonas replied, his voice barely audible. "He changes locations all the time. Last I heard, he had a place near Gothenburg, but that was weeks ago. He could be anywhere."

Erik exchanged a glance with Lars. They finally had a name, a motive, and a witness who could tie Axel Bergström to the murder. But tracking down a man as elusive as Axel would be a challenge.

“You’ve done the right thing by talking to us,” Erik said, rising from his seat. “But you’re not safe. We’ll arrange protective custody for you until we find Axel.”

Jonas nodded weakly, his face pale. “You don’t understand. Axel doesn’t stop. If he knows I’ve talked to you, he’ll come for me.”

“We’ll be ready for him,” Erik replied firmly. “And when he does, we’ll make sure he doesn’t walk away.”

The Attempted Break-in

The protective custody arrangements were swift. Jonas was escorted to a secure location under police supervision, but Erik couldn't shake the uneasy feeling that they were racing against the clock. Axel Bergström wouldn't hesitate to eliminate anyone who threatened his operation, and Jonas had just painted a target on his back.

Erik sat at his desk, the dim light of his office casting shadows over the files spread before him. Lars entered with two steaming cups of coffee, setting one down in front of Erik.

"Anything new?" Lars asked, slumping into the chair opposite him.

"Nothing useful," Erik replied, rubbing his temples. "Jonas' story checks out so far, but we're no closer to Axel. Every lead we've had on him has gone cold."

Lars took a sip of his coffee, his gaze drifting to the case board. "What about that land deal Jonas mentioned? If Axel wanted Karl out of the way for it, there has to be a trail."

Erik's eyes narrowed. "That's a good point. Let's pull property records, financial transactions, anything that ties Axel and Karl to the same deal."

It didn't take long for the pieces to start coming together. By late evening, Erik and Lars had unearthed documents linking both men to a proposed real estate project on the outskirts of Smögen. The land was valuable, close to the water, and zoned for development.

"Here," Lars said, pointing to a highlighted section of a contract. "Karl owned part of this land, but Axel had been pushing to buy him out for months. Karl refused—said he didn't trust Axel's intentions."

"And now Karl's dead," Erik said grimly. "Convenient for Axel, isn't it?"

"Convenient doesn't mean proof," Lars countered.

Erik nodded, but his gut told him they were closing in on something significant. He picked up the phone and called Ingrid, hoping the forensic analysis might reveal another piece of the puzzle.

"Ingrid," Erik said when she answered. "Any progress on the fingerprints we found on Jonas' boat?"

"Yes," she replied, her tone brisk. "We ran them through the database again. Aside from Jonas', we found a partial match for Axel Bergström. It's not enough for an arrest, but it confirms he was there."

"That's something," Erik said. "Keep digging. We need more."

He hung up and looked at Lars. "We have Axel tied to the boat and to Karl's murder. Now we just need to find him."

Later that night, the phone rang again. Erik answered, his heart racing when he recognized the voice on the other end—it was one of the officers stationed at Jonas' safehouse.

"Sir, we've got a situation," the officer said. "There was an attempted break-in about twenty minutes ago. Whoever it was got away, but they knew what they were doing. Silent, efficient. No sign of Jonas, though—he's still safe."

"Do you think it was Axel?" Erik asked, already grabbing his coat.

"Could've been," the officer replied. "We found a note at the scene. It was taped to the window."

"What did it say?"

The officer hesitated before replying. "It said, 'You can't protect him.'"

Erik's grip tightened around his phone. "Stay with Jonas. Double the guard if you have to. I'll be there in twenty minutes."

He hung up, his jaw clenched as he turned to Lars. "Axel's making his move. If we don't act fast, this is going to end badly."

"What's the plan?" Lars asked, already on his feet.

"We use Jonas to draw Axel out," Erik said. "But this time, we'll be ready."

Chapter 4: Trapped by the Tide

The cold wind whipped across the darkened streets as Erik and Lars raced toward the safehouse. The air inside the car was thick with tension, the weight of Axel's threat hanging over them. Jonas was their only link to the elusive criminal, and Axel knew it.

When they arrived, two officers were stationed outside, their hands gripping their weapons tightly as they scanned the area. Erik stepped out of the car, his coat billowing in the wind.

"Status?" he asked one of the officers.

"Quiet so far," the officer replied. "But whoever tried to break in was good. No sound, no real trace. Just the note."

Erik nodded, motioning for Lars to follow him inside. The safehouse was a nondescript building on the outskirts of town, its modest appearance masking the high security measures within. Jonas was sitting in a small living room, his face pale and drawn, his hands shaking as he held a cup of coffee.

"He's going to kill me," Jonas said as soon as Erik walked in. "You can't stop him. You don't know what he's capable of."

"You're still alive, aren't you?" Erik replied calmly. "That means he's not as unstoppable as you think."

Jonas shook his head, his eyes wide with fear. "He doesn't fail. If he came here, it's because he already has a plan."

"And so do we," Erik said firmly. "You're safer here than you would be anywhere else. Trust me."

Lars pulled Erik aside. "This is bad," he muttered. "If Axel's willing to risk a direct confrontation, it means he's desperate—or he's confident he can outmaneuver us."

"We can't afford to wait for him to make the next move," Erik said. "We need to draw him out."

The plan was simple but risky. Jonas would make a public appearance—a carefully staged visit to his boat at the marina. The move was designed to bait Axel into revealing himself, forcing him to act before he could plan another silent strike.

The following morning, Jonas stood at the dock, flanked by two undercover officers posing as dockworkers. Erik and Lars watched from a discreet vantage point, their eyes scanning the crowd for any sign of Axel.

The minutes ticked by, the tension mounting. Jonas shifted nervously, his eyes darting to every passerby. "This isn't going to work," he muttered, barely moving his lips.

"Just stay calm," Erik's voice crackled through the small earpiece Jonas wore. "If Axel's watching, he won't want to wait long."

A shadow moved at the edge of the harbor, catching Erik's attention. He nudged Lars, pointing toward a figure that lingered near a stack of crates. The man's face was obscured by a cap and a scarf, but his movements were deliberate, his attention fixed on Jonas.

"That's him," Lars whispered.

"Wait," Erik said, his voice low. "Let him make the first move."

The figure moved closer, weaving through the crowd. Jonas tensed visibly, his shoulders stiff as the man approached. Then, without warning, the man veered sharply toward the water, disappearing behind a row of boats.

"Damn it, he's running!" Lars said, already moving.

Erik followed, weaving through the narrow pathways between the boats. The suspect was fast, his footsteps echoing on the wet docks. Erik caught a glimpse of him as he rounded a corner, his heart pounding as he closed the distance.

The chase ended abruptly at the edge of the pier. The suspect turned, pulling a knife from his pocket, the blade glinting in the morning light.

"Stay back!" the man shouted, his voice sharp and desperate.

"Drop the knife," Erik said, his weapon trained on the man.

"Leave me alone!" the man yelled, his hands trembling.

"You're not going anywhere," Erik replied, his voice steady.

The man hesitated, his gaze flickering to the water below. Then, with a sudden motion, he lunged toward the edge, throwing himself into the icy waves.

"Damn it!" Erik shouted, running to the edge of the pier. The water churned, but the man was gone, swallowed by the mist and cold.

"Do you think it was Axel?" Lars asked, catching up.

Erik stared at the water for a moment before shaking his head. "No. Just one of his pawns. But Axel knows we're closing in. He won't stay hidden for long."

The failed attempt to capture the suspect at the harbor had only strengthened Erik's resolve. Axel Bergström was testing their limits, gauging how far they were willing to go to stop him. Now, more than ever, Erik knew they had to act decisively.

Back at the station, Erik and Lars pored over their growing collection of evidence. Axel's network was vast, but every piece of information they uncovered brought them closer to dismantling it. The key was finding the missing link—something that would expose his operation and force him into the open.

"Ingrid called," Lars said, breaking the silence. "She's finished analyzing the documents we found in Söderberg's cabin. There's a pattern in the transactions—money flowing through offshore accounts tied to a shell company. She thinks it's how Axel's been funding everything."

"And the land deal?" Erik asked, glancing up from his notes.

"It's tied to the same accounts," Lars replied. "If we follow the money, we might be able to pinpoint where Axel's hiding."

Erik stood, the gears in his mind turning. "Let's get everything to financial crimes. If Axel's been sloppy, there might be a paper trail leading right to him."

The breakthrough came late that afternoon. An investigator from the financial crimes unit confirmed that several recent transactions from the shell company matched activity in a small coastal town near Gothenburg. Axel had been using the funds to lease a warehouse—a perfect place for someone to operate unnoticed.

"Got him," Lars said, dropping the report on Erik's desk.

Erik studied the address, his jaw tightening. "If Axel's there, we have to assume he's not alone. He'll have backup, and he'll be prepared."

"Then we need to be more prepared," Lars replied.

That evening, Erik assembled a team. Officers from neighboring precincts joined the operation, each one briefed on Axel's dangerous history. The plan was meticulous: surround the warehouse, cut off all exits, and bring Axel in alive—if possible.

The convoy of unmarked police vehicles rolled into the quiet coastal town under the cover of darkness. The warehouse loomed ahead, its silhouette stark against the dim glow of the streetlights. Erik and Lars moved with their team, their weapons drawn as they approached the building.

A faint light glimmered through the cracks in the warehouse doors. Erik motioned for silence, signaling two officers to take position by the side entrance.

Inside, faint voices could be heard, punctuated by the sound of something metallic being dragged across the floor. Erik signaled again, his hand tightening around his weapon.

On his mark, the team moved. The doors burst open, the sound of boots on concrete echoing through the cavernous space.

"Police! Don't move!" Erik shouted, his voice cutting through the chaos.

Several figures scattered, their shadows darting in every direction. Axel was among them, his face set in a grim scowl as he bolted toward a stack of crates.

"Stop, Axel!" Lars yelled, chasing him.

Axel didn't stop. He climbed the crates with surprising agility, leaping to a narrow ledge above. Erik followed, his movements careful but relentless.

"You're cornered!" Erik shouted, his voice reverberating through the warehouse. "There's nowhere to go!"

Axel turned, his eyes cold and calculating. “You have no idea what you’re dealing with,” he said, his voice low and venomous.

“Drop the act, Axel,” Erik replied, his weapon trained on him. “It’s over.”

Axel smirked. “Not yet.”

With a sudden motion, Axel leapt from the ledge, landing hard on the floor below. The impact stunned him for a moment, giving Lars just enough time to tackle him to the ground.

“Got you,” Lars growled, snapping handcuffs onto Axel’s wrists.

Axel didn’t struggle. Instead, he laughed—a chilling, hollow sound that echoed through the warehouse. “You think this changes anything?” he said. “You’ve won nothing.”

Erik stepped forward, his eyes locked on Axel’s. “You’re done. And once we unravel your operation, so is everyone you’ve been protecting.”

Axel’s smile faded, but the cold defiance in his eyes remained.

Axel's arrest marked a critical turning point, but Erik knew the battle was far from over. The warehouse raid had revealed the scale of Axel's operations, yet the pieces of the puzzle remained fragmented. Back at the station, the team began the meticulous process of cataloging the evidence. Crates of documents, ledgers, and vials of unidentified substances filled the evidence room, each one a potential key to unraveling Axel's empire.

Jonas was brought to the station under heavy guard. His pale complexion and trembling hands betrayed the fear still coursing through him. Erik wasted no time, escorting him to the interrogation room where Lars was already waiting.

"You've got one chance, Jonas," Erik said, his tone firm. "Axel's in custody, but we need to know everything. If you hold back, we won't be able to protect you."

Jonas nodded hesitantly, his voice trembling as he spoke. "I told you everything I know about Karl. Axel... he didn't tell me much about his other operations. He's careful—compartmentalizes everything. But I do know one thing: he's working with someone bigger."

Erik leaned forward, his brow furrowing. "Bigger? Who?"

Jonas shook his head. "I don't know a name, but it's someone with serious money. Axel always said they were the reason he could afford to take risks. He called them 'the patron.'"

"The patron," Lars repeated, exchanging a glance with Erik.

"Where do we start looking?" Erik asked.

"There's a safehouse," Jonas replied, his voice barely above a whisper. "Not far from the cliffs where Karl... died. Axel used it for meetings with people he didn't trust to come to his main operations. I've never been inside, but I've dropped him off there a few times."

"Do you think this patron ever visited the safehouse?" Lars asked.

Jonas hesitated. "I think so. Axel always made a big deal about keeping it off the radar."

Later that evening, Erik and Lars approached the location Jonas described. The safehouse was nestled among jagged cliffs, its dark silhouette almost invisible against the rocky terrain. The only sound was the crash of waves far below.

"This place is a fortress," Lars muttered as they exited the car.

"That's why Axel liked it," Erik replied, scanning the area with his flashlight. "Let's see if it lives up to its reputation."

The detectives moved cautiously, their weapons drawn. The path to the entrance was treacherous, the ground slick with seawater and loose stones. Erik's flashlight beam landed on a steel-reinforced door, partially concealed by overgrown vegetation.

"Looks like Jonas was telling the truth," Erik said.

He motioned for Lars to cover him as he tried the door. It was locked, but the scratches around the lock suggested it had been forced open recently.

"Someone's been here," Lars observed.

Inside, the air was damp and heavy, carrying the faint smell of mildew. The safehouse consisted of a single room with a table, a few chairs, and a metal cabinet pushed against the wall. Papers and empty coffee cups littered the table, suggesting the place had been used recently.

Lars moved to the cabinet, his gloved hands carefully opening it. Inside were several manila folders, each one marked with cryptic labels: **"Exports," "Acquisitions," "Project Tide."**

"Project Tide?" Lars said aloud, pulling out the folder. He flipped it open, revealing blueprints, handwritten notes, and photographs of coastal areas.

"This isn't just smuggling," Erik said, scanning the documents. "This looks like they were planning something big."

Lars held up one of the photographs. "This is Smögen," he said, pointing to a familiar coastline.

"They weren't just using the town as a cover," Erik muttered. "They were targeting it."

Project Tide

The discovery of the "Project Tide" folder shifted the investigation into high gear. Erik and Lars wasted no time transporting the evidence back to the station, their minds racing with questions. What was Axel planning in Smögen? Why target the coastal town? And who was the mysterious "patron" funding it all?

Back at the station, Ingrid joined them in the evidence room. Her sharp eyes scanned the documents as Erik and Lars recounted their findings.

"Project Tide," Ingrid murmured, flipping through the blueprints and notes. "This isn't just smuggling. It's coordinated, and it's big. Look at this—maps of Smögen's harbor, shipping routes, and coastal structures. They're planning something specific."

"What's their endgame?" Lars asked, leaning over the table.

Ingrid pointed to a set of annotations on one of the maps. "These points are marked along the cliffs and the harbor. If I'm reading this right, they're positioning equipment here, here, and here—likely for underwater operations. It's not clear exactly what they're doing, but it involves the coastline itself."

Erik's brow furrowed as he studied the map. "Could it be illegal fishing, smuggling, or something else entirely?"

"Whatever it is, it's sophisticated," Ingrid replied. "And expensive. That's where the patron comes in. Axel doesn't have the resources for this alone."

Lars tapped the table. "We need to find out who's bankrolling this. If we can expose the patron, Axel's operation collapses."

Hours later, Erik received a call from the financial crimes unit. The lead investigator confirmed a breakthrough—an offshore account tied to Axel's shell company had just been accessed. The location of the transaction: Gothenburg.

"Looks like the patron's making moves," Lars said as Erik hung up.

"Or Axel's people are trying to cover their tracks," Erik replied. "Either way, we follow the money."

By dawn, Erik, Lars, and a small team were en route to Gothenburg. The address tied to the transaction was a luxury high-rise overlooking the harbor. As they approached the building, Erik's phone buzzed with a message from Ingrid:

"Found something else. The equipment noted in Project Tide isn't just for smuggling. It's for extraction—mineral extraction. They're targeting something under the seabed."

Erik's grip on the phone tightened as he relayed the information to Lars. "This isn't just about money. If they're mining minerals illegally, the environmental impact alone could devastate Smögen's coastline."

"Great," Lars muttered. "So now we're dealing with eco-criminals too."

The high-rise was eerily quiet as Erik and Lars approached the penthouse. Two officers flanked the door, their weapons drawn. Erik nodded, and one of them knocked sharply.

"Police! Open up!"

A tense silence followed before footsteps approached the door. It opened just wide enough for a man in a tailored suit to appear. His expression was calm, almost amused.

"Can I help you?" he asked, his voice smooth.

"Police," Erik said firmly, holding up his badge. "We're here to ask you a few questions about your financial connections to Axel Bergström."

The man's smile didn't waver. "I have no idea who that is."

"Then you won't mind if we take a look around," Lars said, stepping forward.

The man hesitated, his calm facade slipping for a moment. “This is highly irregular. I’ll need to contact my lawyer.”

“You can do that,” Erik replied. “After we’re done.”

Erik pushed the door open, motioning for the officers to enter. The penthouse was immaculate, its minimalist decor hiding any obvious signs of criminal activity.

But then Lars spotted it—a laptop sitting on the kitchen counter, its screen displaying a file directory labeled **“Project Tide.”**

“Well, that’s convenient,” Lars said, gesturing to the laptop.

The man’s composure broke as he lunged for the device, but Erik intercepted him, slamming him against the wall.

“That’s enough,” Erik said coldly. “We’re taking you and this laptop in.”

Back at the station, the confiscated laptop from the penthouse proved to be a treasure trove of information. As Ingrid worked on decrypting the files, Erik and Lars began piecing together what was rapidly shaping up to be one of the largest criminal conspiracies they had ever encountered.

“Project Tide isn’t just about Smögen,” Ingrid announced, her eyes glued to the screen as lines of code scrolled past. “It’s a test run. They’re using the town as a prototype for larger operations.”

“What kind of operations?” Lars asked, leaning over her shoulder.

Ingrid brought up a series of detailed schematics. “Underwater mining,” she explained. “They’re targeting rare minerals located in the seabed. These operations aren’t just illegal—they’re catastrophic for the environment. Smögen is their first target because of its unique geological features.”

“Let me guess,” Erik said, crossing his arms. “The patron stands to make billions off this.”

"Easily," Ingrid replied. "If this goes unchecked, they'll be able to replicate it across other coastal areas."

Lars frowned. "What about Axel? He's not smart enough to orchestrate something like this on his own."

"You're right," Ingrid said, pulling up a financial ledger. "Most of the money trail points back to the patron. Whoever they are, they're the mastermind."

As the hours passed, Erik and Lars reviewed the evidence, connecting dots and building their case. The documents from the laptop revealed a network of companies, shell accounts, and operatives spread across Europe. But one name kept resurfacing—a shipping magnate named Karl Björk, known for his investments in high-risk ventures.

"Björk," Lars muttered, tapping the name on the screen. "It fits. He has the resources, the connections, and the reputation for shady dealings."

"If it's him, we'll need more than suspicion to bring him in," Erik said.

Their discussion was interrupted by a knock on the door. An officer entered, his face grim.

"We have a situation," he said. "Jonas was being transferred to another location, but the transport was ambushed."

"What?" Erik shot to his feet. "Is he alive?"

"Barely," the officer replied. "He's in the hospital now. Two of our men didn't make it."

Lars cursed under his breath. "This was Axel's doing, wasn't it?"

"Or the patron's," Erik said, his voice tight. "They're tying up loose ends."

Erik and Lars rushed to the hospital, where Jonas was under heavy guard. His face was pale, a bandage wrapped around his head, and his breathing labored. But his eyes opened when Erik leaned over him.

"Jonas," Erik said softly. "You're safe now, but we need your help. Who ambushed the transport?"

Jonas winced, his voice barely audible. "It wasn't Axel. It was... someone else. They wore masks, but I heard them talking. They mentioned Björk. He... he knows I talked."

Erik exchanged a look with Lars. "That confirms it."

"We need to move fast," Lars said. "If Björk's cleaning up, he won't stop with Jonas."

Jonas' hand weakly grasped Erik's arm. "You have to stop him," he whispered. "If you don't... more people will die."

"You've done your part," Erik said, gripping his hand firmly. "Now it's our turn."

Back at the station, Erik called an emergency meeting. The pieces were falling into place, but the clock was ticking. They had enough evidence to launch a full-scale operation against Björk, but they needed to act before he could disappear.

"Here's the plan," Erik said, addressing the room. "We coordinate with Interpol. Björk's operations span multiple countries, and we'll need their resources to shut him down. At the same time, we put every available officer on tracking Axel's remaining network. If we take out both of them, we can stop this before it spreads."

The room buzzed with urgency as officers prepared for the coordinated operation. Lars leaned over to Erik as the meeting ended.

"Do you think we can pull this off?" Lars asked.

"We have to," Erik replied, his jaw set. "For Jonas. For Smögen. And for everyone else they're planning to destroy."

Chapter 5: The Patron's Web

The early morning fog clung to the streets as Erik and Lars prepared for the operation. Interpol agents, local officers, and specialized units had joined forces to take down Karl Björk. The coordinated effort was the largest operation Smögen had ever seen, a testament to the gravity of the crimes they were about to expose.

Erik stood in the mobile command center, the hum of activity around him a constant reminder of the stakes. Maps of Björk's properties were pinned to a board, red circles marking key locations. The focus of the operation was Björk's private estate outside Gothenburg, a sprawling mansion that served as the nerve center of his operations.

"Everyone in position?" Erik asked, his voice steady despite the tension in his chest.

"Team Alpha is ready to breach the main estate," an Interpol agent replied. "Team Bravo has the dockyards covered. If he tries to escape by water, we'll intercept him."

Erik nodded, turning to Lars. "Once we're inside, we focus on securing Björk and his records. We can't let anything slip through the cracks."

Lars smirked. "Just another day at the office."

Erik managed a tight smile, but his focus never wavered. "Let's move."

The convoy of vehicles approached the estate under the cover of darkness. The sprawling grounds were surrounded by high walls and state-of-the-art security. Infrared cameras and motion detectors dotted the perimeter, but the police had been prepared.

As the teams moved into position, Erik watched from a vantage point near the rear entrance. Through his binoculars, he could see the faint glow of lights in the mansion's upper windows.

"He's there," Lars muttered, crouched beside him. "Lights are on. He doesn't know we're coming."

"Let's keep it that way," Erik replied.

On Erik's signal, the operation began. Team Alpha moved on the front gate, cutting the power to the estate's security systems while Team Bravo secured the dockyards. The crackle of radios and muffled footsteps filled the air as the teams breached the estate.

Inside, the opulence of the mansion was jarring—a stark contrast to the criminal enterprise it hid. Chandeliers sparkled overhead, and plush rugs muffled the sounds of movement. Erik led his team down a hallway lined with paintings, his weapon raised as they approached a heavy wooden door.

"Office," Erik whispered. "This is where he keeps the records."

One of the officers stepped forward, using a battering ram to break the lock. The door swung open, revealing a room filled with filing cabinets, computer monitors, and stacks of documents.

"Secure everything," Erik ordered.

As the team worked, Erik scanned the room. His eyes landed on a wall safe, partially concealed behind a large painting. "Lars, over here," he said.

Lars moved to the safe, pulling a small tool kit from his bag. It took him only minutes to crack it open. Inside was a trove of hard drives, passports, and a ledger that Erik immediately recognized from the files on Project Tide.

"This is it," Erik said, holding up the ledger. "Everything we need to tie Björk to Axel and the patron network."

A crash echoed from the hallway, followed by shouts. Erik's hand flew to his weapon as he moved toward the door.

"Status?" he barked into his radio.

"Contact in the east wing!" came the reply. "Possible escape attempt!"

"Lars, stay here and secure the evidence," Erik ordered, already moving toward the source of the commotion.

In the east wing, Erik found chaos. Officers were in pursuit of a figure darting through the corridors, their footsteps echoing off the marble floors. Erik caught a glimpse of the man—a slim figure in a dark suit, moving with the precision of someone trained to evade capture.

"It's Björk!" an officer shouted.

Erik sprinted after him, his pulse pounding in his ears. Björk led them to a side door that opened onto the estate's gardens, where the cold night air bit at Erik's face.

"Stop!" Erik yelled, his weapon raised.

Björk hesitated, glancing back with a smirk. "You're too late, detective," he said.

Erik's finger hovered over the trigger, but before he could act, Björk turned and ran toward a waiting speedboat at the dock.

"Bravo team, he's heading to the water!" Erik shouted into his radio.

The roar of the speedboat's engine filled the air as Björk leapt aboard and accelerated toward open water. Team Bravo sprang into action, their boats in pursuit as Erik watched from the shore.

"Do you think they'll catch him?" Lars asked, appearing beside Erik.

“They have to,” Erik replied, his voice grim. “But even if he gets away, we have enough to dismantle his operation. He can’t hide forever.”

The chase on the water unfolded like a scene from a high-stakes thriller. Björk’s speedboat cut through the icy waves, its engine roaring as it sped toward the open sea. Team Bravo followed in swift pursuit, their boats trailing him closely.

Erik and Lars listened to the radio chatter from the shore, their breaths visible in the frosty air.

“Bravo One, we’ve got visual!” one of the officers called out. “He’s heading south, increasing speed!”

“Intercept him before he gets too far,” Erik said into his radio.

The police boats fanned out, cutting off Björk’s escape routes. The roar of engines mixed with the crashing waves, and a spotlight from one of the patrol boats illuminated Björk’s vessel.

“Pull over, Björk!” an officer shouted through a loudspeaker. “You have nowhere to go!”

But Björk didn’t stop. Instead, he veered sharply toward a cluster of rocks jutting out of the water, attempting to outmaneuver his pursuers.

“He’s trying to lose them,” Lars muttered, his eyes fixed on the chase.

“Let’s hope the team knows what they’re doing,” Erik replied grimly.

One of the police boats sped ahead, cutting across Björk’s path. The maneuver forced him to slow down just enough for the trailing boats to close the gap.

“Got him!” Bravo One reported. “We’re moving in!”

Moments later, a loud crash echoed over the water as Björk's boat collided with one of the rocks. The impact sent him sprawling across the deck, and his engine sputtered to a stop.

"Suspect down!" Bravo One confirmed. "Moving to apprehend!"

Erik let out a breath he hadn't realized he was holding. "Good work, Bravo Team. Bring him in."

The Interrogation

At the station, Björk was escorted into the interrogation room under heavy guard. His suit was disheveled, his hair damp from the spray of the sea, but his defiance was unshaken. He sat down, his eyes narrowing as Erik and Lars entered.

"I assume you're here to gloat," Björk said, his voice dripping with disdain.

"No," Erik replied, his tone calm but firm. "We're here to hold you accountable."

Björk smirked. "For what, exactly? You don't have anything solid. A few files, some vague connections. It won't hold up in court."

"Funny you mention that," Lars said, placing the recovered ledger and hard drives on the table. "Because we have everything we need. Financial records, communications, even witness statements tying you to Project Tide."

Björk's expression faltered for a brief moment before his smug demeanor returned. "You think you've won, but you're playing a dangerous game. Do you have any idea who you're dealing with?"

Erik leaned forward, his gaze steady. "We know exactly who we're dealing with. And we're taking your entire operation down, piece by piece."

Björk laughed, but there was an edge of desperation in it. "You can't stop this. It's bigger than me. Bigger than you. If you think arresting me will change anything, you're deluding yourselves."

"Maybe," Erik said, his voice cold. "But it's a start."

The arrest of Karl Björk sent shockwaves through Smögen and beyond. News of his capture dominated the headlines, with reporters speculating about the scale of his criminal enterprise. For Erik, it was a small victory, but he knew the battle was far from over. The shadow of the patron loomed larger than ever, and

Björk's defiance during the interrogation only solidified Erik's resolve to bring the entire operation to its knees.

Back at the station, Ingrid continued combing through the recovered files, her focus unwavering. Erik and Lars joined her, the tension in the room palpable.

"Anything new?" Erik asked, his voice laced with impatience.

Ingrid nodded, her finger hovering over a series of encrypted emails. "These are from Björk's personal account. It's taking time to decode, but I've already found references to another shipment—scheduled for tomorrow night."

"Where?" Lars asked, leaning closer.

Ingrid brought up a map on her screen. "A private dock near Stockholm. It's heavily secured, which makes sense if this is part of Project Tide."

"Do we know what they're shipping?" Erik pressed.

"Not yet," Ingrid replied. "But based on the equipment logs and the patterns we've seen, it's likely tied to the underwater mining operations. This could be their final setup before going fully operational."

Erik exchanged a glance with Lars. "If this is their last piece, we need to move now. Contact Interpol and get a team ready."

The Breach

The next evening, Erik and Lars found themselves at the outskirts of Stockholm, overlooking the private dock. Floodlights illuminated the area, casting long shadows over the rows of containers and heavy machinery. Security guards patrolled the perimeter, their movements precise and coordinated.

"This place is a fortress," Lars muttered, peering through binoculars.

"Which means whatever's here is valuable," Erik replied. "We'll have one chance to get it right."

The team moved into position, each officer briefed on the high stakes of the operation. As Erik gave the signal, the units advanced, moving silently through the shadows.

The breach was swift and calculated. Officers overwhelmed the guards at the gate, their movements synchronized and efficient. Erik and Lars led the charge toward the main warehouse, their weapons drawn as they entered the cavernous space.

Inside, the scale of the operation became clear. Stacked crates bore labels in multiple languages, their contents unknown. In the center of the warehouse stood a massive cylindrical device, its purpose immediately obvious to Erik.

"That's drilling equipment," he said, his voice low. "They're ready to extract."

Before he could process further, a shout echoed through the warehouse.

"Hands up!"

Erik turned to see a group of armed men stepping out from behind the machinery. One of them held a rifle, his finger hovering near the trigger.

"Drop your weapons!" the man barked.

Erik exchanged a glance with Lars, who gave a subtle nod. Slowly, they lowered their weapons to the ground.

"You've got no idea what you're dealing with," the man continued, his voice cold.

"Actually, we do," Erik said calmly. "You're part of a criminal network responsible for environmental destruction and smuggling operations across Europe. And now, you're done."

The man laughed, but it was hollow. "You think arresting us will stop this? We're just the beginning. The patron has plans far beyond Smögen or Stockholm."

"Then we'll stop him too," Erik replied.

The standoff ended as more officers stormed the warehouse, their presence overwhelming the remaining guards. The armed men surrendered one by one, their defiance melting under the weight of the operation's failure.

Erik and Lars began examining the crates, opening one to reveal high-grade industrial tools and hazardous materials. Ingrid arrived moments later, her laptop in hand.

"This confirms it," she said, pointing to her screen. "These shipments were meant for the seabed extraction sites. If we hadn't stopped this, they'd already be operational."

Lars let out a low whistle. "We got lucky."

"No," Erik said, his tone firm. "We worked for this. And we're not done yet. Let's get everything cataloged. The more evidence we have, the harder it'll be for the patron to recover."

The bust at the Stockholm dockyard had brought Erik and his team closer to understanding the full scale of Project Tide. With Björk in custody and critical evidence from the site secured, they finally had a clearer picture of the operation's mechanics. But one glaring question remained unanswered: who was the patron?

Back at the station, the interrogation room was dimly lit, the air thick with tension. Björk sat across from Erik and Lars, his smug demeanor showing cracks after hours of relentless questioning.

"Tell us about the patron," Erik demanded, his voice steady.

Björk chuckled dryly. "Do you think I'd sell out someone like that? Even if I did, you wouldn't be able to touch them."

"Try us," Lars said, leaning forward.

"You're so naive," Björk replied, shaking his head. "The patron isn't just a person—it's a network. Corporations, governments, people you'd never suspect. You take me down, another one steps in. That's how this works."

Erik leaned in, his gaze piercing. "You think you're untouchable because you've surrounded yourself with powerful people. But every network has a weak link. Keep talking, and maybe we'll find yours."

For the first time, Björk's confidence wavered. He looked at Erik, his smirk fading. "If I talk, they'll kill me."

"If you don't talk," Erik countered, "you'll rot in prison while they keep profiting. Your choice."

Björk hesitated, the weight of his decision evident in his eyes. Finally, he leaned back in his chair, his voice dropping to a whisper.

"There's a name," he said. "Someone who connects it all. Magnus Ekström."

Erik's brow furrowed. "Ekström? The industrialist?"

Björk nodded. "He's more than that. He's the one funding the mining technology, the shipping routes, everything. Without him, the operation collapses."

The revelation set off a flurry of activity at the station. Ingrid dove into Ekström's background, uncovering layers of business dealings, offshore accounts, and suspicious partnerships. As the pieces fell into place, a pattern emerged—Ekström wasn't just the patron; he was the architect of Project Tide.

"Look at this," Ingrid said, pointing to her screen. "Ekström's companies are tied to every facet of this operation. Shipping, extraction, even political lobbying to keep environmental protections weak. It's all connected."

Erik studied the data, his mind racing. "Where is he now?"

Ingrid hesitated before answering. "According to his travel records, he's in Smögen. He owns a private estate just outside of town. It's secluded, heavily secured."

"That's where we go next," Erik said, his tone resolute.

By evening, Erik, Lars, and a team of officers were en route to Ekström's estate. The sprawling property sat atop a hill overlooking the sea, its towering gates and high-tech security a testament to Ekström's wealth and paranoia.

As the team approached, Erik gave the signal to cut the power to the estate. The grounds were plunged into darkness, and the officers moved in under the cover of night.

The main house was eerily quiet as Erik and Lars led the breach. Inside, the opulence mirrored Björk's mansion, but the air was heavy with a sense of abandonment. Rooms were empty, desks cleared, and computers wiped.

"He knew we were coming," Lars muttered, scanning the room with his flashlight.

"Or someone warned him," Erik replied.

They searched the estate methodically, finding only fragments of documents and empty safes. But as they reached the basement, Ingrid's voice crackled through Erik's radio.

"I'm picking up a signal," she said. "There's a hidden server room below ground. Find it."

In the basement, Erik spotted a wall panel slightly out of place. With a sharp pull, it revealed a concealed doorway leading to a narrow staircase. At the bottom, they found the server room—a high-tech setup with blinking lights and screens displaying encrypted data.

"Looks like Ekström left us a parting gift," Lars said as Ingrid arrived with her laptop.

"I'll need time to decrypt this," Ingrid said, already connecting her equipment.

Erik's gaze hardened. "Do whatever it takes. This might be our last chance to stop him."

The server room's hum filled the narrow basement as Ingrid's fingers flew across her keyboard. The encrypted files on Magnus Ekström's hidden server were a treasure trove, but every passing second felt like an eternity. Erik and Lars stood nearby, their eyes darting between the door and Ingrid's screen. The threat of an ambush loomed over them, and time was not on their side.

"This is it," Ingrid said suddenly, her voice tense. "I'm in. These files contain detailed blueprints for the underwater mining operations and financial records linking Ekström to Project Tide. He's not just funding this—he's orchestrating it."

"Anything that tells us where he is now?" Erik asked.

Ingrid nodded, scrolling rapidly. "There are logs of recent communications. Ekström's last message suggests he's heading to an offshore platform—likely the heart of the operation."

"Coordinates?" Lars pressed.

"Sending them to your phone now," Ingrid replied. "But you won't have much time. If he's there, he'll be preparing to disappear."

Erik clenched his jaw. "We'll take care of it. Secure the data and get it to Interpol. We're going after him."

The offshore platform loomed on the horizon like a mechanical behemoth. As the police boat cut through the waves, Erik and Lars prepared for what would undoubtedly be a dangerous confrontation. The platform's lights blinked ominously against the night sky, and the distant sound of machinery grew louder as they approached.

"This is it," Erik said, pulling on his gear. "If Ekström gets away, we lose everything."

"We won't let that happen," Lars replied, checking his weapon.

The team boarded the platform under the cover of darkness, their footsteps muffled against the steel grates. The air was thick with the smell of oil and salt, and the rumble of machinery vibrated beneath their feet.

Erik motioned for silence as they moved through the labyrinth of pipes and catwalks. They encountered minimal resistance at first—two guards taken down swiftly and quietly. But as they reached the central control room, the tension snapped like a wire.

"Freeze!" an armed guard shouted, stepping into their path.

The team scattered for cover as gunfire erupted, bullets sparking against the metal walls. Erik pressed his back to a column, signaling Lars to flank the attackers.

Lars moved swiftly, taking out one of the guards with a precise shot. The remaining assailants faltered, their confidence waning as the police advanced. Within minutes, the firefight was over, the guards disarmed and restrained.

"Control room's clear," Lars said, his breathing heavy.

Erik nodded, stepping over the fallen guards. The room was a maze of monitors and controls, each screen displaying real-time data on the mining operation. But the chair at the center of the room was empty.

“He’s not here,” Lars said, scanning the room.

Erik’s radio crackled. “Sir, we found a helipad on the upper deck. There’s a chopper warming up.”

“Ekström,” Erik muttered. “He’s making his escape.”

Chapter 6: A Reckoning at Sea

The offshore platform trembled under the rumble of the helicopter's rotors. The sound reverberated through the steel beams as Erik and Lars raced toward the upper deck. The cold wind bit at their faces, the salt spray from the waves below adding a sharp sting. Every second counted; Magnus Ekström was moments away from escaping.

When they reached the helipad, the helicopter's engine roared to full power. The sleek black chopper began to lift, its rotors slicing through the dark sky. Ekström was visible through the open side door, shouting orders to the pilot as he climbed aboard.

"Ekström! Stop!" Erik shouted, his voice cutting through the din.

Ekström turned, his face illuminated by the harsh floodlights. His expression was defiant, but his eyes betrayed a flicker of fear.

"You're too late!" he yelled back, gripping the doorframe of the helicopter. "You think this ends with me? You've stopped nothing!"

"Not if we stop you here!" Lars shouted, raising his weapon.

The helicopter lurched, hovering just above the platform as the pilot prepared to fly. Erik's eyes locked on a cable tethering the helicopter to a nearby railing. With a split-second decision, he grabbed the cable and yanked with all his strength.

The chopper tipped violently, the sudden jolt throwing Ekström off balance. He stumbled, his hand slipping from the doorframe as he fell hard onto the platform's deck.

"Move in!" Erik barked, charging forward as Lars covered him.

Ekström scrambled to his feet, his gaze darting between the officers closing in on him and the helicopter still hovering above. "You can't do this!" he shouted, backing away. "I'll have every lawyer in the country—"

"Shut it," Lars growled, grabbing Ekström's arm and forcing him to the ground.

"Cuff him," Erik ordered, stepping back as Lars secured Ekström's wrists. The helicopter pilot, seeing his passenger subdued, cut the engine and raised his hands in surrender.

As the adrenaline faded, Erik stood over Ekström, his breathing heavy. The industrialist's once-imposing presence had crumbled; he was just another criminal now, his grandiose plans reduced to nothing.

"You're finished," Erik said coldly. "Your operation, your network—it's all over."

Ekström glared up at him, his defiance still flickering. "You think you've won? You've only delayed the inevitable. There will always be someone ready to take my place."

"Maybe," Erik replied, his voice steady. "But not today."

Back at the station, the victory was palpable. Ekström's arrest marked the culmination of months of painstaking work, and the evidence recovered from the platform was overwhelming. Ingrid worked tirelessly to catalog the data, her reports providing the final nail in the coffin for Project Tide.

"We've got him," she said, her voice tinged with exhaustion but satisfaction. "There's enough here to dismantle his entire network and ensure he never sees daylight again."

"Good," Erik said, leaning against the table. "But let's not celebrate just yet. There's still work to do."

Lars smirked. "Always the optimist."

Erik allowed himself a faint smile. "It's not about optimism. It's about making sure we've got all the pieces. People like Ekström don't act alone. We need to find out who else was involved."

Ekströms Empire

The next few weeks were a blur of arrests, investigations, and courtroom battles. Ekström's empire crumbled under the weight of the evidence, and his collaborators—politicians, executives, and enforcers—were brought to justice one by one.

But as the dust settled, Erik couldn't shake the feeling that the victory was incomplete. The patron network had taken a hit, but the machine itself wasn't destroyed. He knew it was only a matter of time before someone else stepped in to fill the void.

"You look like you need a drink," Lars said one evening, finding Erik staring out over the water near the pier.

Erik chuckled softly. "Maybe I do. But there's still so much we don't know. Ekström might be behind bars, but this isn't over."

Lars clapped him on the shoulder. "It never is. But today, we've done enough. Let's leave tomorrow's fight for tomorrow."

Erik nodded, the weight on his shoulders feeling just a little lighter. For now, at least, they had won.

The victory on the platform was decisive, but the weight of the operation lingered with Erik. As the team returned to the station, Magnus Ekström remained silent, his defiance replaced by a calculating glare. Erik couldn't ignore the warning Ekström had given—about the size and resilience of the network they had just begun to dismantle.

In the station's evidence room, Ingrid was already sifting through the massive haul of data recovered from the platform's servers. Hard drives, encrypted communications, and financial records painted a vivid picture of the global operation.

"This is bigger than we thought," Ingrid said, her voice grim. "Ekström's platform wasn't just a mining site—it was a command hub. It coordinated operations across multiple countries."

"Do we have any leads on his partners?" Erik asked, leaning over her screen.

"Several," Ingrid replied, pulling up a series of names. "These are key players—bankers, shipping magnates, and even politicians. But this one..." She pointed to a name highlighted in red. "...is someone we need to focus on. Johan Ström, a logistics tycoon. Most of the equipment and personnel went through his companies. He's the next link in the chain."

Erik exchanged a glance with Lars. "If Ström is as entrenched as Ekström, this won't be easy."

"It never is," Lars replied with a wry smile.

The next morning, Erik and Lars prepared to move on Johan Ström. The evidence was compelling enough for a warrant, and a coordinated team was already en route to Ström's headquarters in Malmö. The glass-fronted skyscraper towered above the city, its pristine exterior belying the corruption beneath.

Inside, the team fanned out, moving swiftly to secure the premises. Erik and Lars headed for Ström's office on the top floor, their footsteps muffled by the plush carpet.

When they entered, Ström was waiting. A tall, imposing man in a tailored suit, he sat behind a mahogany desk, his hands clasped in front of him.

"Detectives," Ström said smoothly, his voice calm. "To what do I owe the pleasure?"

Erik stepped forward, his badge in hand. "We have a warrant to search these premises and take you into custody. You're under investigation for your role in Project Tide."

Ström's expression didn't falter. Instead, he leaned back in his chair, a faint smile tugging at his lips.

"You're making a mistake," he said. "Whatever you think you've uncovered, I assure you, it's a misunderstanding."

"Misunderstanding?" Lars interjected, placing a folder on the desk. "These are financial records directly linking your companies to illegal mining operations. Care to explain?"

Ström glanced at the folder but didn't open it. "I think I'll wait for my lawyer."

The search of Ström's office and servers yielded more than Erik had anticipated. Hidden among legitimate business records were contracts, coded communications, and evidence of substantial kickbacks to high-ranking officials.

The Network

Back at the station, Ingrid analyzed the findings. "Ström was a key facilitator," she said. "He handled logistics, laundering money and ensuring smooth operations for Ekström's network. Without him, they lose their ability to move equipment and personnel effectively."

"Then we've dealt a major blow," Erik said, though his tone remained cautious. "But there's still more out there. Every time we cut one head off, two more seem to grow back."

"That's the nature of organized crime," Lars replied. "But we're getting closer to the root."

As the day drew to a close, Erik found himself standing on the station's rooftop, the city lights stretching out before him. The victory against Ekström and Ström was significant, but the knowledge of the network's scale weighed heavily on his mind.

Lars joined him, a bottle of beer in hand. "You're thinking too much again," he said, offering Erik the bottle.

Erik accepted it with a faint smile. "Hard not to. We've done a lot, but there's so much left to do."

Lars clinked his bottle against Erik's. "One step at a time, partner. We'll get there."

Erik nodded, the weight easing just slightly. For now, they had struck a meaningful blow against the shadows. And tomorrow, they would face whatever came next.

Johan Ström's arrest sent a ripple effect through the criminal network tied to Project Tide. As news of his capture spread, the names of additional collaborators began to surface, each new revelation drawing Erik and his team deeper into the labyrinth of corruption. But while the operation had dealt significant blows, the fight was far from over.

Ingrid worked late into the night, piecing together a comprehensive map of connections from the recovered data. Her desk was covered with printouts, photographs, and files, all linked by strands of red thread that crisscrossed a large bulletin board.

"This is incredible," she said, gesturing to the board as Erik and Lars approached. "Ström was just one piece. These people—corporate executives, corrupt officials, and international financiers—make up the rest of the puzzle."

Erik studied the board, his eyes narrowing as he focused on a cluster of names near the center. "This name keeps showing up: Henrik Löfgren. Who is he?"

Ingrid tapped a document on her desk. "Löfgren is an investment banker with ties to offshore accounts used to fund Project Tide. If we follow his money trail, it might lead us to the network's core."

"Do we know where to find him?" Lars asked.

Ingrid nodded. "He's in Oslo. I've already forwarded his details to Interpol, but we'll need to act quickly if we want to catch him before he disappears."

Erik exchanged a glance with Lars. "Looks like we're heading to Oslo."

Norway

The trip to Norway was swift but tense. Erik and Lars, accompanied by two Interpol agents, arrived in Oslo with a clear mission: apprehend Henrik Löfgren and secure the financial records tying him to the patron network.

The target was a high-rise in the city's financial district. Löfgren's office was on the top floor, a polished, modern space that reflected his wealth and influence. The team entered the building under the guise of business visitors, their movements precise and deliberate.

"Top floor," Erik said as they stepped into the elevator. His voice was calm, but his grip on his sidearm betrayed the tension beneath.

When the elevator doors opened, the team moved quickly, securing the exits and converging on Löfgren's office. Inside, the banker stood behind a glass desk, his expression a mixture of shock and indignation as the officers entered.

"What is this?" Löfgren demanded, raising his hands. "You have no right—"

"We have every right," Erik interrupted, holding up his badge. "Henrik Löfgren, you're under arrest for your involvement in Project Tide."

As Lars secured the banker, Erik scanned the office. A sleek computer sat on the desk, its screen displaying financial charts and encrypted files.

"Ingrid will want to see this," Erik muttered, motioning to one of the agents to secure the computer.

Back in Sweden, the data extracted from Löfgren's computer proved invaluable. Ingrid's analysis revealed layers of financial transactions that extended far beyond Project Tide. The network had ties to illegal activities ranging from arms trafficking to political bribery.

“This isn’t just about mining,” Ingrid said, her voice heavy with disbelief. “This network is funding global corruption on a scale I’ve never seen.”

Erik nodded, his expression grim. “And Löfgren was managing the finances for all of it. Have we found anything that connects directly to Ekström?”

Ingrid pointed to a transaction log on her screen. “This payment here—eight million euros—went from Ekström’s accounts to a shell company Löfgren set up. It’s the missing link.”

Lars leaned against the desk, his arms crossed. “So we’ve got the money trail. What about the other players? Any names we can move on?”

“Plenty,” Ingrid replied. “But this one stands out: Sofia Nyström. She’s a lobbyist in Brussels, and based on these communications, she was instrumental in keeping environmental regulations weak to protect the mining operations.”

Erik sighed. “It never ends, does it?”

“No,” Ingrid said. “But with Löfgren and Ekström in custody, the network is weaker than it’s ever been.”

“Where is Sofia Nyström now?” Lars asked.

Ingrid checked her notes. “She’s in Brussels. Based on her schedule, she’s attending a private gala tonight. It’s the perfect chance to bring her in without a public scene.”

“Then we move,” Erik said.

In Brussels, the ornate ballroom of the gala shimmered under crystal chandeliers. Wealth and influence mingled effortlessly as high-powered individuals sipped champagne and discussed global affairs. Amidst the crowd, Sofia Nyström stood out, her elegant gown and composed demeanor exuding power.

Erik and Lars, dressed in formal wear, blended into the gathering. Their eyes tracked Nyström as she moved from group to group, her laughter and charm masking the role she played in the criminal network.

"She doesn't suspect a thing," Lars murmured, his voice low as he sipped from a glass of water.

"She won't see it coming," Erik replied, slipping a small communication device into his ear.

As Nyström moved toward the exit, Erik signaled Lars. They intercepted her just as she stepped into the quiet hallway outside the ballroom.

"Sofia Nyström?" Erik said, flashing his badge.

Her smile froze, and a flicker of recognition crossed her face. "Yes? Can I help you?"

"You're under arrest for your involvement in Project Tide," Erik said calmly.

"This is outrageous!" Nyström hissed, her composure cracking as Lars secured her hands. "Do you have any idea who I am?"

"We do," Lars replied dryly. "That's why you're coming with us."

Back in Sweden, Nyström's arrest was another critical victory. The files recovered from her possessions revealed direct communications with Magnus Ekström and Johan Ström, further solidifying the case against the network.

"These people were running an empire," Ingrid said, pointing to a timeline on her computer screen. "Nyström wasn't just lobbying. She was brokering deals and coordinating with other players to protect the network's interests."

"And now she's going to answer for it," Erik said, his voice firm.

The momentum from the recent arrests culminated in a series of coordinated raids across Europe. Police dismantled shipping operations in Rotterdam, froze assets in Zurich, and shut down smuggling routes in the Balkans. With each success, the network's grip weakened, but Erik knew the fight wasn't over.

Late one evening, he stood by the harbor in Smögen, watching the moonlight dance on the waves. Lars joined him, a familiar bottle of beer in hand.

"You should really find another way to relax," Erik said with a faint smile.

"I'll consider it," Lars replied, offering Erik the bottle. "But you know, we've done something good here. We've stopped something that could've gotten a lot worse."

Erik nodded, the weight of their accomplishments sinking in. "We've made a dent. That's all we can do."

Lars clinked his bottle against the railing. "Here's to more dents."

Erik chuckled, the sound carried away by the wind. For the first time in months, he allowed himself a moment of peace, knowing that tomorrow would bring another battle.

Chapter 7: Shadows in the Fog

The glow of dawn illuminated the harbor in Smögen as Erik stood on the pier, watching the fishing boats return with their morning haul. The scene was tranquil, but his mind was restless. The recent arrests had crippled Project Tide, but Erik knew the network was like a hydra—cut off one head, and two more would grow in its place.

Behind him, Lars approached, a steaming cup of coffee in hand. "You're up early," Lars said, handing Erik the cup.

"Couldn't sleep," Erik replied, taking a sip. "Too much to think about."

"Let me guess," Lars said, leaning against the wooden railing. "You're wondering if we actually made a difference."

Erik nodded. "We've stopped a lot of people, but there's always someone waiting to take their place. Ekström, Ström, Nyström—they're all pieces of something much bigger."

"True," Lars admitted. "But that doesn't mean we haven't made progress. Every piece we take out weakens the whole."

Erik sighed, his gaze fixed on the horizon. "I just wonder if we'll ever see the end of it."

Later that morning, Erik and Lars arrived at the station to find Ingrid waiting for them. Her expression was grim, and her usual energetic demeanor was subdued.

"We've got a problem," she said, leading them into the evidence room.

"What kind of problem?" Erik asked, his tone wary.

Ingrid pulled up a series of encrypted communications on her computer. "These came from the data we recovered from Löfgren's and Nyström's files. I've been decrypting them all night.

It looks like there's another player involved—someone higher up than Ekström."

"Higher than Ekström?" Lars said, his brow furrowing. "I thought he was the top of the chain."

"So did I," Ingrid replied. "But these messages suggest otherwise. There's someone referred to as 'The Broker.' They're coordinating operations across multiple countries, and they're the one keeping the network alive."

"Do we have anything on them? A name? A location?" Erik asked.

"Not yet," Ingrid admitted. "But there's a meeting scheduled in Copenhagen tomorrow night. If The Broker is as important as they seem, they might be there."

Erik exchanged a glance with Lars. "Then that's where we'll be."

The following evening, Erik and Lars arrived in Copenhagen, their presence concealed by the bustling crowds of the city. The meeting was set to take place at a secluded warehouse on the outskirts of the harbor—a fitting location for a clandestine gathering.

As they approached, the air was thick with tension. The warehouse loomed in the shadows, its windows darkened. Erik signaled for silence as they positioned themselves near the entrance.

Inside, muffled voices could be heard, the words indistinct but filled with urgency. Erik glanced at Lars, his expression firm. "This is it. We go in quiet, secure the area, and find The Broker."

"Got it," Lars replied, his weapon drawn.

They moved swiftly, entering through a side door and slipping into the shadows. The warehouse was vast, its interior filled with crates and scattered papers. In the center of the room, a group of individuals stood around a table, their faces partially obscured by the dim light.

Erik's eyes locked on a figure at the head of the table. They were dressed sharply, their posture commanding. "That has to be The Broker," Erik whispered.

Lars nodded. "We take them now?"

"Not yet," Erik said. "We need to hear what they're saying. Get closer."

As they crept forward, The Broker's voice became clearer. "Our recent losses are setbacks, but they're not the end. We've faced worse before, and we've always rebuilt. This time will be no different."

Erik's grip tightened on his weapon. The Broker's confidence was unnerving, their tone filled with a cold determination.

But before they could get closer, one of the guards spotted them. "Intruders!" he shouted, reaching for his weapon.

Chaos erupted. The group scattered, and The Broker bolted toward a back exit. Erik and Lars gave chase, dodging gunfire as they pursued the figure through the maze-like warehouse.

"Don't let them get away!" Erik shouted, his voice cutting through the cacophony.

Lars fired a warning shot, the bullet ricocheting off a metal beam near The Broker. The figure stumbled, their path briefly interrupted, but they recovered quickly and sprinted toward a waiting car outside.

"Stop!" Erik yelled, but The Broker was already climbing into the vehicle.

The engine roared to life, and the car sped off, disappearing into the night.

The Broker

Copenhagen's harbor was shrouded in fog as Erik and Lars positioned themselves near the warehouse where the meeting was supposed to take place. The air was damp and cold, the sounds of the bustling city a faint hum in the distance.

In the shadows, they waited, listening intently to the muffled voices emanating from within the warehouse. Erik's heart raced as he recognized the authoritative tone of the figure they suspected to be The Broker.

"This is it," Erik whispered to Lars. "If The Broker is here, we can finally bring down the rest of the network."

Lars nodded, adjusting his grip on his weapon. "We'll make it count."

As they moved silently toward the side entrance, the sound of footsteps from behind made them freeze. Erik turned sharply, his weapon drawn, but relaxed slightly when he recognized the approaching Interpol agents.

"We've secured the perimeter," one of the agents said. "No one gets in or out without us knowing."

"Good," Erik replied. "Let's move."

Inside, the warehouse was a maze of crates and machinery, the dim light casting long shadows across the concrete floor. At the center of the space, a group of individuals gathered around a table covered with maps and documents. The figure at the head of the table exuded authority, their sharp suit and commanding posture leaving no doubt that this was The Broker.

Erik signaled for the team to spread out, each officer taking position to ensure no one could escape. The tension was palpable as they edged closer, their steps silent.

“Tonight, we rebuild,” The Broker said, their voice calm but resolute. “What we’ve lost is insignificant compared to what we’ll gain. This is not the end—it’s just the beginning.”

Erik felt a surge of anger. These people had caused untold damage, and here they were, planning their next move as if nothing had happened. He raised his weapon and stepped into the light.

“Police! Don’t move!” he shouted, his voice echoing through the warehouse.

The room erupted into chaos. The individuals around the table scattered, some reaching for weapons while others bolted for the exits.

“Lars, cover the exits!” Erik barked as he advanced on The Broker.

The Broker didn’t run. Instead, they stood calmly, their hands raised but their expression unfazed. “Detective Erik Johansson,” they said smoothly. “I’ve heard so much about you.”

“Then you know why we’re here,” Erik replied, his weapon trained on them.

“Yes,” The Broker said with a faint smile. “But you’re too late. The network is bigger than you can imagine, and cutting me down won’t stop it.”

The sound of gunfire echoed from the other side of the warehouse as the team engaged with the fleeing suspects. Lars’s voice crackled through Erik’s radio. “We’ve got runners heading for the east exit. Two down, but we need backup!”

“Hold your position,” Erik replied before turning back to The Broker. “Get on the ground, now!”

The Broker hesitated, their smile fading as Erik took a step closer. Suddenly, they lunged toward a hidden panel on the table. Erik reacted instinctively, firing a warning shot that stopped The Broker in their tracks.

"I said, on the ground!" Erik repeated, his voice cold.

The Broker slowly knelt, their movements deliberate. As Lars and another officer arrived to secure the scene, Erik felt the weight of the moment settle over him.

"We've got them," Lars said, cuffing The Broker's hands.

"For now," Erik muttered. He couldn't shake the feeling that this victory was temporary—that somewhere, someone else was already preparing to take The Broker's place.

The operation in Copenhagen had been a success, but the fallout was just beginning. Back at the station in Smögen, Erik stood with Ingrid and Lars as they reviewed the evidence recovered from The Broker's meeting. Boxes of documents and hard drives were stacked on tables, each piece a potential key to dismantling the remnants of the network.

"This is bigger than I thought," Ingrid said, her voice low as she sifted through the files. "The Broker wasn't just coordinating Project Tide—they were involved in smuggling, financial fraud, even human trafficking."

Erik ran a hand over his face, exhaustion etched into his features. "It always gets worse, doesn't it?"

"It does," Lars replied, leaning against the table. "But at least we've got them. That's one less player pulling the strings."

Ingrid tapped on her laptop, bringing up a series of encrypted files. "There's more. The Broker kept detailed communications with other high-ranking figures. These files mention a 'Council'—a group overseeing operations across Europe. The Broker wasn't the head. They were just another cog in the machine."

Erik's stomach tightened. "A council? How many more layers does this thing have?"

“At least five key players, based on these files,” Ingrid said. “But their identities are hidden. If we’re going to bring them down, we’ll need to dig deeper.”

Amsterdam

The next few days were a blur of coordinated efforts. Interpol agents worked alongside Erik's team to track down leads from the recovered data. Each arrest chipped away at the network, but the elusive Council remained out of reach.

One night, Erik sat alone in his office, poring over a map of Europe pinned to the wall. Red pins marked locations tied to the network, their web sprawling across borders.

"You're going to drive yourself crazy staring at that," Lars said, stepping into the room with two mugs of coffee.

Erik accepted the mug with a faint smile. "It feels endless. Every time we get closer, something else comes up."

"That's how these things work," Lars said, taking a seat. "But we've done more in the past few weeks than most people do in years. You can't forget that."

"I know," Erik replied, his voice heavy. "But I can't shake the feeling that we're still just scratching the surface."

Lars nodded, sipping his coffee. "One step at a time, partner. That's all we can do."

A breakthrough came days later. Ingrid's relentless work on The Broker's encrypted files uncovered a lead—a safe house in Amsterdam that the Council had used for meetings. It was a long shot, but Erik and Lars wasted no time assembling a team to raid the location.

The safe house was a nondescript building on a quiet street. As the team approached, Erik's pulse quickened. If this was another dead end, it could cost them the momentum they had worked so hard to build.

"Stay sharp," Erik said as they breached the door.

The interior was sparse but meticulously organized. Maps and documents covered the walls, each one bearing connections to the network's operations. In the center of the room was a desk, and on it sat a laptop, its screen glowing faintly.

"Ingrid's going to love this," Lars said, motioning to the computer.

Erik nodded, already scanning the room for anything that could lead them closer to the Council. "Bag everything. We're taking it all."

Back in Smögen, Ingrid dove into the new trove of evidence with her characteristic intensity. Days turned into nights as she decrypted files and pieced together connections. Finally, she called Erik and Lars into her office, her expression a mix of excitement and urgency.

"I've got something," she said, spinning her laptop around to show them.

The screen displayed a network of names and locations, each one tied to the Council. "This is it. These are the people we've been looking for. They're operating under aliases, but we've matched their patterns to real identities."

Erik leaned closer, his heart pounding. "Who are they?"

Ingrid pointed to the screen. "Five individuals. Politicians, executives, and one military official. They're spread across Europe, but they coordinate everything—funding, logistics, even recruitment."

Lars let out a low whistle. "We just hit the jackpot."

"But this won't be easy," Erik said, his voice steady. "These people have resources, influence. They won't go down without a fight."

"Which is why we need to move fast," Ingrid said. "If they catch wind of this, they'll disappear."

Erik nodded. "Then let's get to work."

The revelations about the Council ignited a frenzy of activity. Erik and Lars coordinated with Interpol, setting up simultaneous operations across multiple countries to take down the high-ranking individuals identified in Ingrid's files. Each member of the Council represented a crucial piece of the network, and their capture would deliver a devastating blow to the operation.

Ingrid worked tirelessly, providing real-time updates as Erik and Lars led their teams. Every new piece of information brought them closer to dismantling the Council's infrastructure. But as the hours turned into days, the pressure began to mount.

"We've got a lead on one of them," Ingrid announced during a late-night briefing. "Gregor Madsen. He's a logistics magnate based in Hamburg, and according to our sources, he's scheduled to meet with a key operative tomorrow afternoon."

"Do we know the location?" Erik asked.

"A private yacht docked in the Hamburg marina," Ingrid replied. "If we move quickly, we can catch him before he leaves."

"Let's make it happen," Erik said, his determination unwavering.

The marina was eerily quiet as Erik, Lars, and their team approached the target. The yacht loomed in the distance, its sleek design a stark contrast to the shadowy dealings it concealed.

"Everyone in position?" Erik whispered into his radio.

"Ready," came the responses from the team members scattered around the dock.

With a nod from Erik, the team moved in. The sound of their footsteps was muffled by the damp wooden planks as they boarded the yacht. Inside, the luxury was overwhelming—crystal chandeliers, leather seating, and polished wood paneling. But Erik's focus remained sharp as they cleared each room.

In the main cabin, they found Gregor Madsen. He sat at a table covered in documents, his expression shifting from shock to fury as Erik and Lars entered.

“Gregor Madsen,” Erik said, his voice steady. “You’re under arrest for your role in Project Tide.”

“You don’t know what you’re doing,” Madsen spat, his hands clenched into fists. “This won’t stop anything.”

“We’ll see about that,” Lars replied as he secured Madsen’s wrists.

The Turning Point

Back at the station, Madsen's arrest proved to be a turning point. The documents recovered from his yacht revealed critical details about the Council's operations, including hidden accounts, offshore assets, and encrypted communications with other members.

"These files are gold," Ingrid said, scrolling through the data on her laptop. "They connect Madsen directly to the Council's financial network. And more importantly, they point to our next target—Anastasia Petrova, a political fixer operating out of Prague."

Erik's mind raced as he absorbed the information. "What's the timeframe?"

"She's hosting a fundraiser tomorrow night," Ingrid replied. "It's a high-profile event, but we can use that to our advantage. If we move carefully, we can extract her without causing a scene."

Erik nodded. "Then let's keep the momentum going."

The operation in Prague was executed with precision. Erik and Lars infiltrated the event under the guise of attendees, their formal wear blending seamlessly with the glittering crowd. Anastasia Petrova was easy to spot—her commanding presence and polished demeanor drew attention wherever she went.

As she mingled with influential figures, Erik and Lars closed in. Timing was everything, and when the moment was right, they approached her near the bar.

"Ms. Petrova," Erik said, flashing his badge discreetly. "We need to have a word."

Petrova's smile faltered, and her eyes narrowed. "I'm afraid I don't know what this is about," she said, her voice icy.

"You will soon," Lars replied, guiding her toward the exit.

The arrest was swift, and the fallout immediate. Petrova's confiscated devices provided another wealth of information, linking her to bribes, policy manipulations, and coordination with the Council.

Back in Smögen, Erik, Lars, and Ingrid reconvened to assess their progress. With Madsen and Petrova in custody, the Council's power was waning, but the final pieces of the puzzle remained elusive.

"We've done a lot," Lars said, leaning back in his chair. "But there's still more out there."

"And we're not stopping until we get it all," Erik replied.

Ingrid's phone buzzed, drawing her attention. As she read the message, her eyes widened. "You're going to want to see this," she said, turning her laptop toward Erik and Lars.

The screen displayed a new encrypted file from Madsen's yacht. Ingrid had just finished decrypting it, and its contents were chilling—a detailed plan for a massive operation involving all remaining Council members.

"This is it," Erik said, his voice grim. "They're planning something big. And we have to stop them."

The arrest of Anastasia Petrova marked yet another victory, but the deeper Erik and Lars delved into the Council's operations, the more intricate the web became. The documents seized from Petrova's belongings revealed a highly structured network, with each member playing a critical role.

Back in Smögen, Ingrid worked relentlessly to make sense of the sheer volume of data. Her desk was buried under printouts and open files, each one detailing transactions, communications, and operational blueprints.

"There's something we've been missing," Ingrid said, rubbing her temples as Erik and Lars joined her in the evidence room. "All of these members—Ekström, Madsen, Petrova—they're connected, but not directly. There's someone else tying them together."

"Another leader?" Erik asked, his tone sharp.

"More like an overseer," Ingrid replied, pointing to a series of coded emails. "These messages reference someone called 'The Architect.' They've been issuing directives to the Council, orchestrating everything from the shadows."

Lars let out a low whistle. "So, the Council isn't the top. There's someone above them."

"Exactly," Ingrid said. "And based on these files, The Architect is planning something big. A global operation that could undo everything we've worked to stop."

Erik leaned over the desk, his jaw tightening. "Do we have any leads on their identity?"

"Just one," Ingrid replied, opening a satellite image on her laptop. "A private compound in Montenegro. It's heavily fortified, but there's evidence tying it to The Architect. If we're going to stop this, we need to act now."

The flight to Montenegro was tense. Erik, Lars, and their team reviewed the mission details, each officer acutely aware of the stakes. The compound, nestled in a remote valley surrounded by dense forests, was more fortress than home.

"This is going to be a tough one," Lars said, peering out the window as the plane descended.

"It always is," Erik replied, his expression unreadable.

Under the cover of darkness, the team approached the compound. The air was thick with tension as they moved through the trees, their footsteps muffled by the soft earth. In the distance, the compound's lights glowed faintly, the high walls and armed guards a reminder of what they were up against.

“Remember the plan,” Erik whispered. “We breach from the west, disable their communications, and secure The Architect.”

The team split into groups, each one moving with practiced precision. As Erik and Lars led their unit toward the western gate, the sound of a guard’s footsteps made them freeze. Erik signaled for silence, his hand tightening on his weapon.

Moments later, the guard passed, oblivious to their presence. Erik nodded, and the team moved swiftly, cutting through the perimeter fence and slipping inside.

The compound’s interior was a maze of corridors and staircases, each turn revealing more signs of the operation’s scale. Maps and documents covered the walls, while monitors displayed surveillance feeds from locations across the globe.

“This is bigger than we thought,” Lars muttered, scanning the room.

“No time to process,” Erik replied. “Let’s find The Architect.”

Chapter 8: The Final Confrontation

Montenegro's rugged mountains framed the horizon as Erik and Lars prepared for the mission. The private compound, heavily fortified and surrounded by dense forest, was their final target—the lair of The Architect, the mastermind behind the Council. Months of relentless work had led them here, and Erik knew this could be their last chance to dismantle the network completely.

"Everyone knows the plan," Erik said, addressing the team as they huddled behind a ridge overlooking the compound. "We go in quietly, secure The Architect, and gather as much evidence as we can. No mistakes."

Lars nodded, his expression grim. "This is it. Let's end this."

The team moved with precision, using the cover of night to mask their approach. The compound was illuminated by powerful floodlights, their beams cutting through the darkness as guards patrolled the perimeter.

Ingrid's voice crackled through Erik's earpiece. "I've disabled their external cameras, but you'll need to move fast. Backup generators could bring them back online at any moment."

"Understood," Erik replied, signaling for the team to advance.

The western gate was the weakest point in the compound's defenses. Using bolt cutters, Lars swiftly breached the fence, allowing the team to slip inside. The air was tense, every sound amplified as they crept through the shadows toward the main building.

Inside, the compound was a maze of sterile hallways and high-tech security. Erik led the team through each corridor, their steps muffled by the thick carpeting.

"We're close," Ingrid's voice came through the earpiece. "The Architect should be in the central chamber."

As they approached the chamber, the tension was palpable. Erik signaled for the team to fan out, each member taking position to ensure no escape routes were left uncovered.

The chamber door was heavy and reinforced, but a small access panel provided a way in. Ingrid guided Erik through the override process, and within minutes, the door slid open with a mechanical hiss.

Inside, The Architect stood at a large digital console, the glow of multiple screens casting eerie shadows across the room. Data scrolled rapidly across the monitors, each one displaying operations tied to the Council.

"Don't move!" Erik commanded, stepping into the room with his weapon raised.

The Architect turned slowly, their face calm and expressionless. "Detective Johansson," they said, their voice low and measured. "You've been persistent."

"On the ground," Erik ordered, his voice unwavering.

The Architect smirked. "You think arresting me will stop this? The network is already rebuilding. You've delayed us, nothing more."

Lars moved swiftly, securing The Architect's hands behind their back as Erik scanned the room. "Ingrid, we've got them," Erik said into his earpiece. "But there's a lot of data here. We'll need extraction teams."

"I'm on it," Ingrid replied. "Downloading what I can remotely, but you'll need to secure those drives."

The mission's success came with a price. As the team began gathering evidence, an alarm blared through the compound. Guards swarmed toward the chamber, and a fierce firefight erupted.

"Hold them off!" Erik shouted, returning fire as the team formed a defensive perimeter.

The Architect remained silent, their smirk infuriatingly intact as chaos unfolded around them.

“We’ve got what we need!” Lars called out. “Let’s move!”

The team retreated methodically, covering each other as they made their way out of the compound. By the time they reached the extraction point, the first light of dawn was breaking over the mountains.

The Blueprint

Back in Smögen, the evidence recovered from the compound provided the final pieces of the puzzle. Ingrid worked tirelessly to catalog the data, uncovering the full extent of The Architect's plans and the remnants of the Council's operations.

"We've done it," Ingrid said one evening, her voice heavy with exhaustion. "The network is finished."

Erik stood by the window, his gaze distant. "For now," he said softly.

Lars placed a hand on his shoulder. "You've done more than anyone thought possible, Erik. Take the win."

Erik nodded, allowing himself a faint smile. For the first time in months, the weight of the case began to lift.

The firefight at the compound in Montenegro had left its scars, but Erik and Lars pushed forward, determined to see the mission through. As dawn broke over the rugged mountains, the team regrouped at a temporary command center set up nearby. The Architect was securely detained, and the extracted data provided a clearer picture of the network's final threads.

Ingrid's voice came through the radio, crisp but weary. "I'm going through the files now. It's worse than we thought—The Architect wasn't just planning a continuation of the network. They were preparing to expand globally."

"What kind of expansion?" Erik asked, exhaustion weighing heavily on his words.

"Illegal mining in Africa, arms smuggling in the Middle East, and even cyberattacks targeting financial institutions in Europe," Ingrid explained. "This wasn't just about maintaining their operations—it was about growing them into an untouchable empire."

Erik exchanged a glance with Lars, whose jaw tightened. "So, we didn't just stop a network," Lars muttered. "We stopped the blueprint for something much bigger."

"And we're not done yet," Ingrid added. "There are still key operatives in play—people who can pick up where The Architect left off. But this data gives us an advantage. We know who they are."

Back in Smögen, the team worked tirelessly to dismantle the final pieces of the network. The information extracted from The Architect's servers was a goldmine, revealing names, locations, and assets tied to the remaining operatives.

One name stood out: Viktor Luchin, a financier operating out of Zurich. His role was critical, managing the funds that kept the network alive.

"If we take Luchin down, we sever the lifeline," Ingrid said during a briefing. "Without him, the network collapses financially."

"What's our window?" Erik asked.

"We've tracked his movements," Ingrid replied, bringing up surveillance footage on her laptop. "He's scheduled to meet with his associates at a private bank tomorrow afternoon. It's our best shot."

Zurich

Zurich's crisp air and orderly streets were a stark contrast to the chaos Erik and Lars had experienced in Montenegro. The private bank stood tall among the city's skyline, its polished glass façade reflecting the late afternoon sun.

"This place screams untouchable," Lars muttered as they approached the building.

"Not today," Erik replied, adjusting his jacket.

The team entered the bank under the guise of clients. Their movements were calculated, each step bringing them closer to Luchin's meeting room. When they reached the floor, Erik signaled the team to take their positions.

Inside the meeting room, Luchin was deep in conversation with two associates. The sight of the officers bursting through the door froze him in place.

"Viktor Luchin," Erik said, his tone cold. "You're under arrest for your role in Project Tide."

Luchin's face twisted into a sneer. "You think this will stop anything? Money moves faster than you can."

"We'll see about that," Lars replied, placing cuffs on his wrists.

The arrest of Viktor Luchin marked the beginning of the end. Without his financial backing, the remnants of the network began to crumble. Ingrid's analysis of his seized accounts led to further arrests, each one bringing them closer to full dismantlement.

But Erik knew there was still more to uncover. One evening, as he sat in his office reviewing reports, a knock on the door pulled him from his thoughts. Lars entered, holding two bottles of beer.

"You're overthinking again," Lars said, placing a bottle in front of Erik.

"I can't help it," Erik replied with a faint smile. "We've done a lot, but I can't shake the feeling we're missing something."

Lars shrugged, taking a sip of his beer. "Maybe. Or maybe, for once, we actually finished the job."

Erik chuckled softly. "Maybe."

The dismantling of the Council was celebrated as a victory, but Erik's instincts told him their fight wasn't over. As Ingrid sifted through the last of the decrypted files from The Architect and Viktor Luchin, she uncovered a chilling detail—a name that hadn't appeared in any previous investigations: Emil Algren.

"He's not on any records we've looked at before," Ingrid said, her voice laced with unease. "But these documents suggest he's been operating as a shadow figure, possibly coordinating a backup plan for the network."

"Where is he now?" Erik asked, leaning over her desk.

Ingrid brought up a satellite image on her screen. "Algren owns a private island off the coast of Norway. It's heavily fortified, but it seems to be a staging ground for something major. There's activity there—ships coming and going, high-tech equipment being moved in."

Lars stepped into the room, his expression grim. "So, this Emil Algren is the failsafe? If we don't stop him, the whole thing could start over?"

"That's exactly what it looks like," Ingrid replied.

Erik straightened, his determination hardening. "Then we need to move. We can't let him rebuild what we've taken down."

The Island

The journey to Norway was swift, but tension hung heavy in the air. Erik and Lars reviewed the mission briefing with their team, knowing this would be their most challenging operation yet. Algren's island was surrounded by treacherous waters and equipped with advanced surveillance and defenses.

As their boat approached the island under the cover of night, Erik's voice cut through the radio. "Everyone stay sharp. This could be our last chance to stop them for good."

The team navigated the rough waters, their small vessel nearly invisible in the darkness. When they reached the island's shore, they disembarked quickly, using the cover of the rocky terrain to stay hidden.

The compound on Algren's island was sprawling, a labyrinth of high-tech facilities surrounded by dense forest. As Erik and Lars led their team through the underbrush, they could see guards patrolling the perimeter, their flashlights cutting through the gloom.

"We take this slow and quiet," Erik whispered. "No alarms. We get Algren, and we secure whatever he's working on."

The team split into smaller units, each tasked with disabling key elements of the compound's defenses. Erik and Lars moved toward the main facility, their movements deliberate and silent.

Inside, the facility was a hive of activity. Technicians worked at computers, and crates marked with untraceable labels were being loaded onto vehicles. Erik's heart pounded as he realized the scale of Algren's operation.

"They're mobilizing," Lars muttered. "We need to move fast."

In the central control room, Emil Algren stood at the helm, overseeing his operation with a calm authority. The room was a stark contrast to the chaos outside—clinical, organized, and eerily quiet.

Erik and Lars entered swiftly, their weapons raised. “Emil Algren,” Erik said, his voice steady. “You’re under arrest.”

Algren turned slowly, his expression unflinching. “Detective Johansson,” he said, a faint smile playing on his lips. “I wondered how long it would take you to find me.”

“Hands up. Now,” Erik ordered.

“You think this is over?” Algren asked, raising his hands slowly. “You’ve only scratched the surface. The Council, The Architect, even me—we’re nothing compared to what’s coming.”

“What’s coming?” Lars demanded, stepping closer.

Algren smirked. “You’ll find out soon enough.”

As Lars secured Algren, Erik moved to the control panels, scanning the screens. One monitor displayed a live feed of a cargo ship departing from the island, its hold filled with equipment.

“Ingrid, do you see this?” Erik said into his earpiece.

“I see it,” Ingrid replied. “That ship is carrying something big. If it gets out of Norwegian waters, we’ll lose it.”

Erik’s jaw tightened. “We’re not done yet.”

The team split up—half stayed behind to secure the compound while Erik and Lars pursued the ship in a commandeered vessel. The chase through the icy waters was harrowing, the waves crashing against their boat as they closed in on the fleeing ship.

When they finally reached the vessel, Erik and Lars boarded under cover of darkness. The ship’s deck was a maze of containers, and the sound of the waves masked their footsteps as they moved toward the bridge.

Inside, the crew was subdued quickly, their resistance no match for Erik's team. Lars secured the ship's manifest, his eyes widening as he read it.

"Erik, this isn't just equipment," Lars said. "They've been transporting materials for weapons manufacturing. High-tech stuff, enough to arm an army."

Erik's blood ran cold. "We need to bring this ship back. If this cargo gets into the wrong hands..."

"It won't," Lars replied firmly.

Back in Smögen, the successful capture of Emil Algren and the seizure of the cargo ship marked the true end of the network. Ingrid's analysis of the ship's contents revealed the scope of what could have been—a global threat that would have undone everything they had fought for.

"We've stopped it," Ingrid said, her voice tinged with both relief and exhaustion. "For now, at least."

Erik stood at the station's window, watching the waves crash against the shore. "It's never really over," he said softly.

Lars joined him, a faint smile on his face. "Maybe not. But for once, we've done enough."

Erik nodded, his shoulders relaxing for the first time in months. For now, the storm had passed.

The capture of Emil Algren and the seizure of the cargo ship brought a sense of closure to months of relentless pursuit. But Erik knew that the network's shadowy reach had left scars on all of them. The Smögen station buzzed with activity as Ingrid, Lars, and the team pieced together the final threads of evidence, ensuring there was no room for the Council's remnants to regroup.

Erik stood by the evidence board, now nearly bare. The once intricate web of names, locations, and operations had been dismantled piece by piece. Only a few strands remained, but they felt less like threats and more like ghosts—shadows of what had been.

"Everything points to Algren being the last link," Ingrid said, her voice steady but exhausted. "With him in custody and the cargo ship secured, we've cut off their resources, their leadership, and their infrastructure."

Lars leaned against the desk, arms crossed. "Feels like the end, doesn't it?"

Erik's gaze lingered on the board. "It feels like we've done everything we could. But you know as well as I do—there's always something left."

Later that night, Erik found himself on the pier, the salty breeze brushing against his face as he stared at the dark water. The weight of the case still clung to him, even as he tried to convince himself it was over.

Lars appeared beside him, a familiar bottle of beer in hand. "Thought I might find you here," he said, offering Erik the bottle.

"You always seem to know," Erik replied with a faint smile, taking the beer.

"Years of practice," Lars said, leaning against the railing. "So, what's next for you?"

Erik exhaled, the question catching him off guard. "I don't know," he admitted. "I've been chasing this for so long, I don't remember what it's like not to."

Lars nodded, his expression thoughtful. "Maybe it's time you figured that out. You've earned a break, Erik. We all have."

Erik glanced at Lars, then back at the horizon. "Maybe you're right. But it's hard to let go."

“You don’t have to let go,” Lars said. “Just take a step back. Let the world spin without you for a while.”

The next morning, the Smögen station felt quieter than usual. The buzz of urgency had been replaced with a calm efficiency as the team prepared their final reports. Ingrid sat at her desk, her laptop glowing with the last traces of decrypted data.

“This is it,” she said as Erik and Lars entered the room. “The final report is ready. Every piece of evidence, every name, every connection—it’s all here.”

Erik nodded, his gratitude evident. “You’ve done more than anyone could’ve asked for, Ingrid.”

She smiled faintly, the weight of the case showing in her tired eyes. “We all have.”

Lars clapped Erik on the shoulder. “So, Captain, what’s the plan? Do we celebrate? Sleep for a week?”

Erik chuckled. “Maybe both.”

The culmination of their efforts came in the form of a press conference. The arrests, the evidence, and the dismantling of the Council were announced as a resounding success. The world would never know the full extent of what they had stopped, but for Erik and his team, the victory was enough.

As the cameras flashed and reporters shouted questions, Erik stepped back, letting the moment belong to those who had worked tirelessly beside him.

Lars approached, his grin wide. “Not your scene, is it?”

Erik shook his head. “Never has been.”

“Let’s get out of here,” Lars said. “We’ve got better things to do.”

Erik nodded, a sense of peace washing over him for the first time in months. Together, they left the chaos behind, ready to face whatever came next.

Chapter 9: A Fragile Peace

The days following the dismantling of the Council felt surreal. For the first time in months, Erik woke up to a quiet phone and a clear sky. The urgency that had driven him and his team through sleepless nights and high-stakes missions had evaporated, leaving behind a strange void.

Smögen had returned to its calm, coastal rhythm. Fishing boats dotted the harbor, and the smell of salt and seaweed filled the air. But Erik couldn't quite let himself relax. As he walked the familiar streets, every shadow felt like a reminder of what they had faced—and what might still be lurking.

"Still on edge?" Lars asked, catching up with Erik near the docks.

Erik smiled faintly. "I guess I don't know how to switch it off."

"You'll figure it out," Lars replied. "Might take some time, but you will."

Back at the station, Ingrid was busy wrapping up the final details of their investigation. The evidence they had collected was being cataloged and sent to international authorities, ensuring that every loose end was tied up.

"These are the last files," she said, handing Erik a flash drive. "Interpol has everything they need now."

"Good work," Erik said. "You've been the backbone of this team, Ingrid. I hope you know that."

She smiled, though exhaustion was evident in her eyes. "Thanks, Erik. But this team wouldn't have gotten anywhere without you and Lars."

Lars entered the room, a cup of coffee in hand. "Are we having a moment here? Should I leave?"

Erik chuckled. "Just finishing up."

“Good,” Lars said. “Because I’ve got an idea. We should celebrate. A real celebration, not just sitting around with paperwork.”

Erik raised an eyebrow. “What do you have in mind?”

“There’s a pub down by the harbor,” Lars said. “Drinks, music, no talk about work. Just for one night.”

Erik glanced at Ingrid, who shrugged. “I’m in,” she said.

The pub was alive with laughter and music when they arrived. For the first time in what felt like years, Erik let himself relax. He and his team shared drinks, stories, and the kind of camaraderie forged in the crucible of danger.

As the evening wore on, Erik found himself staring out at the harbor through the pub’s window. The dark waves glimmered under the moonlight, a reminder of the world beyond their small town.

“You’re thinking again,” Lars said, sliding a fresh drink in front of him.

Erik laughed. “Can’t help it.”

“You’ve earned a break,” Lars said. “Take it.”

Erik nodded, his shoulders easing. For tonight, at least, the shadows could wait.

Der Letter from Interpol

The next morning, the harbor was quiet as Erik walked along the pier. The sea, calm and reflective, mirrored his own shifting thoughts. The weight of the case was lifting, but it left behind questions he wasn't sure how to answer. What was next? Could he truly leave it all behind and embrace the quiet life Smögen offered?

As he reached the end of the pier, Ingrid appeared, her hands tucked into her jacket pockets. "Couldn't sleep?" she asked.

Erik chuckled. "Not much. Just... thinking."

"About?" Ingrid prompted, standing beside him and gazing out at the water.

"Everything," Erik admitted. "We've done so much, but I still feel like there's more out there. Like we've only scratched the surface."

Ingrid nodded. "There's always more. But we don't have to carry it all, Erik. We did what we could, and that has to be enough."

Erik glanced at her, appreciating the wisdom in her words. "You've got a way of putting things into perspective."

"It's a gift," Ingrid said with a smile.

Later at the station, the final pieces of paperwork were being filed. Lars was unusually quiet as he worked, his typical humor subdued. Erik noticed and pulled up a chair next to him.

"Something on your mind?" Erik asked.

Lars shrugged. "I guess I'm just wondering what's next. This case—it was everything for so long. Now it's done, and I'm not sure what to do with myself."

Erik leaned back, considering. "You'll figure it out. We all will. Maybe it's time to focus on something outside of work for a while."

Lars smirked. "Like what? Fishing? Yoga?"

"Who knows?" Erik said with a grin. "Maybe both."

Ingrid entered the room, holding a sealed envelope. "This just came in," she said, handing it to Erik.

Erik opened it, his brow furrowing as he read. It was a letter from Interpol, commending the team for their work and officially closing the case. It also contained offers of new assignments—high-profile cases that needed experienced detectives.

"You thinking about taking it?" Lars asked, noticing the way Erik lingered over the letter.

Erik folded the paper and placed it on the desk. "I don't know. Part of me feels like I should, but another part... I think I need a break."

"Whatever you decide, we're with you," Ingrid said firmly.

Erik nodded, grateful for their support. "Thanks. But for now, I think I'll stay here. Smögen's earned a little peace."

That evening, Erik sat by the fire at home, the letter from Interpol resting on the table beside him. He sipped a cup of coffee, his thoughts shifting between the past and the future. For the first time, he allowed himself to imagine a life beyond the job—a life where the shadows of crime weren't always looming.

The sound of waves crashing against the rocks outside reminded him of the town's enduring rhythm, its steady pace offering a contrast to the chaos he had grown used to.

As the fire crackled, Erik picked up the letter and stared at it for a moment before placing it back on the table. The decision could wait. For now, the peace of Smögen was enough.

Erik spent the next few days settling into the calm that Smögen had to offer. The case files were boxed and archived, the station had returned to its usual rhythm, and for the first time in what felt like an eternity, he allowed himself to embrace the ordinary. Yet, a part of him still felt like a visitor in his own life, as if he didn't quite belong in this newfound stillness.

One afternoon, Erik found himself wandering the harbor, the sound of seagulls and the gentle slap of water against the docks filling the air. He stopped at the local café, where the owner, Greta, greeted him with a warm smile.

"Detective Johansson," she said, setting a cup of coffee in front of him. "It's good to see you out and about. You look... lighter."

Erik chuckled softly. "Maybe I am. The work's finally done—for now, at least."

Greta nodded knowingly. "Good. You've earned it. This town needs people like you to keep it safe, but it also needs you to take care of yourself. You can't pour from an empty cup, you know."

Erik smiled, appreciating her words more than he expected. "Thanks, Greta. Maybe I'll actually take that advice."

Meanwhile, Lars had taken Ingrid's suggestion to "focus on something outside work" literally. Erik spotted him one evening at the harbor, attempting to fish with an old rod and a tangled line.

"Didn't think you were serious about this," Erik said, walking up with a grin.

"Neither did I," Lars admitted, untangling the line. "But you know what? It's kind of nice. Quiet, simple. I could get used to it."

Erik sat on a nearby bench, watching Lars wrestle with the line. "I think that's the idea. Finding something that doesn't remind us of what we've been through."

Lars paused, his expression softening. "We've been through a lot, haven't we?"

"We have," Erik said. "But we came out on the other side. That's what matters."

At the station, Ingrid was preparing to leave for a well-deserved break. She had finally accepted Erik's insistence that she take some time off, though it took a week of persuasion.

"Are you sure you'll survive without me?" she teased as Erik walked her to the door.

"I'll manage," Erik replied with a smirk. "Barely."

Ingrid laughed. "You better. And don't let Lars burn the place down while I'm gone."

"I'll do my best," Erik said. "Enjoy your time off. You've earned it."

As she left, Erik watched the station door close behind her. The quiet that followed felt different—not empty, but peaceful.

That night, Erik stood on the pier once more, the town's lights reflecting on the water. He thought about everything they had accomplished, the lives they had saved, and the shadows they had pushed back. For the first time, he felt a sense of pride—not just in what they had done, but in the team that had made it possible.

Lars joined him, as usual, two bottles of beer in hand. "You're thinking again," he said, handing one to Erik.

"Habit," Erik replied, taking the bottle.

"Well, try thinking about this," Lars said, raising his bottle in a toast. "To us. To the team. And to whatever comes next."

Erik clinked his bottle against Lars's, a genuine smile crossing his face. "To whatever comes next."

As the waves lapped against the shore and the stars dotted the night sky, Erik allowed himself to let go—if only for a little while.

The Calm before the Storm

Erik's days in Smögen began to fall into a comforting routine. Mornings were spent walking along the quiet coastline, afternoons were filled with small tasks at the station, and evenings offered the rare chance to share a meal with friends. The chaos that had dominated his life seemed to drift further into the distance, replaced by a slow, deliberate rhythm that felt almost foreign.

One afternoon, as Erik reviewed minor cases at his desk, a familiar figure appeared in the doorway. It was Ingrid, back from her short leave, looking refreshed but with the determined expression he had come to rely on.

"Miss me?" she asked, stepping into the room.

"Not even a little," Erik replied with a smirk. "How was your break?"

"Too short," Ingrid admitted, dropping a folder on his desk. "But I think I needed it. And I see the station is still standing, so you managed without me."

"Barely," Erik said, flipping open the folder. "What's this?"

"Updates from Interpol," Ingrid explained. "They've been following up on the remnants of the Council. Seems like we hit them hard enough to stop any immediate plans for rebuilding."

"That's good news," Erik said, scanning the report. "So, for now, it's quiet."

"For now," Ingrid echoed.

The station's routine began to settle into something Erik hadn't thought possible: normalcy. The team handled the usual small-town incidents—missing pets, minor disputes, and the occasional speeding tourist. While Erik appreciated the calm, he sometimes felt out of place in this slower pace of life.

One evening, Lars invited Erik and Ingrid to dinner at his home. The modest house near the edge of the forest was warm and welcoming, filled with the scent of roasted fish and freshly baked bread.

"I think this is the first time I've had you both here," Lars said, pouring drinks.

"Probably because you're usually too busy chasing people through warehouses," Ingrid quipped.

Lars laughed. "True. But I figured it was time we had a proper meal, no work, no chaos."

The evening passed in easy conversation and laughter, the kind of simplicity Erik hadn't realized he missed. As they sat around the table, he felt a rare sense of contentment.

"We make a good team," Lars said, raising his glass. "Even if we're not chasing down international criminals anymore."

Erik smiled, clinking his glass against Ingrid's and Lars's. "To the team."

"To the team," they echoed.

As the days turned to weeks, Erik began to find solace in the stillness. The memories of their fight against the Council still lingered, but they no longer weighed him down. Instead, they served as a reminder of what they had achieved—and of the people who had made it possible.

One afternoon, as Erik walked along the pier, he saw Greta from the café waving to him.

"Detective Johansson!" she called, walking over.

"Greta," Erik said, smiling. "How are you?"

"I'm good, but more importantly, how are you?" she asked, her tone curious.

Erik paused, considering her question. "I think I'm finally starting to relax. It's strange, but... nice."

Greta smiled. "You deserve it. And don't let anyone tell you otherwise."

That evening, Erik stood by his window, looking out at the moonlit harbor. The town's quiet rhythm had become something he cherished, a contrast to the chaos he had known for so long. As he sipped his coffee, he thought of the people who had stood by him—Lars, Ingrid, and the entire team.

For the first time in years, Erik allowed himself to believe that maybe, just maybe, he could let go of the need to always be on guard. The world wasn't perfect, but for now, his corner of it felt whole.

The gentle routine of Smögen began to feel like home again for Erik. The days passed without the constant pressure of looming danger, replaced by simple, grounding moments. Yet, in the quiet, Erik found time to reflect—not just on the victories, but on the cost of achieving them.

One morning, as Erik walked along the shore, Lars joined him, coffee in hand.

"Been thinking," Lars began, handing Erik a cup. "All this... quiet. Feels strange, doesn't it?"

Erik nodded, taking a sip of the coffee. "It does. After everything, it feels almost... too quiet."

"Maybe we're just not used to it," Lars said, his gaze fixed on the horizon. "But maybe it's exactly what we needed."

Erik looked at his friend, appreciating the simple truth in his words. "You're right. It's what we fought for. Might as well enjoy it while it lasts."

Back at the station, Ingrid was finishing up her analysis of the last remnants of the Council's communications. She had spent days pouring over encrypted files and cross-referencing names, ensuring nothing was left unchecked.

"I think this is it," she said, calling Erik and Lars into the briefing room. "The final thread."

She gestured to the screen, where a map displayed red dots scattered across Europe. "These are the last known assets tied to the Council. They're small—safe houses, bank accounts, nothing major. But if we leave them, they could be used to rebuild."

Erik studied the map, his jaw tightening. "We've come this far. Let's make sure it's finished."

The team coordinated with Interpol to close the remaining gaps. The last safe houses were raided, the accounts frozen, and the final operatives brought into custody. With every step, Erik felt the weight of the case lifting, replaced by a growing sense of closure.

After the final operation, Ingrid approached Erik, her expression a mix of relief and pride. "That's it," she said. "We've done everything we can."

Erik nodded, a small smile crossing his face. "It feels good, doesn't it?"

"It does," Ingrid agreed. "Now it's up to the rest of the world to keep it that way."

As Smögen settled into winter, the town seemed even more serene. Snow dusted the rooftops, and the harbor was quiet under a pale gray sky. Erik found himself drawn to the pier, where he often stood in silent reflection.

One evening, as the first stars appeared, Lars joined him, as he so often did.

"Do you ever think about what's next?" Lars asked, leaning against the railing.

Erik shrugged. "Sometimes. But I'm trying not to think too far ahead. For once, I want to stay in the moment."

Lars grinned. "Look at you. The great Erik Johansson, learning to live in the moment. I never thought I'd see the day."

Erik laughed. "Neither did I."

That night, as Erik sat by the fire, a letter arrived. It was from Interpol, thanking the team once again for their service and extending another offer for Erik to lead a new task force. Erik read the letter carefully, his thoughts turning to his team and the life he had begun to build in Smögen.

He folded the letter and placed it on the table, a decision forming in his mind. For now, Smögen was where he belonged. The work would always be there, but so would the quiet moments he had come to cherish.

As the fire crackled and the snow fell softly outside, Erik allowed himself a rare sense of peace.

Chapter 10: Back to the Beginnings

Winter deepened in Smögen, cloaking the town in frost and painting the rooftops with a glittering layer of snow. Erik found the stillness of the season fitting—a final chapter to the storm that had consumed so much of the year. As he walked through the narrow streets, the town seemed to breathe with the quiet rhythm of renewal.

At the station, things had settled into a comfortable routine. Ingrid was back to her sharp, efficient self, Lars kept the team's morale high with his steady humor, and Erik felt himself easing into his role as a leader not bound by constant crisis.

"You seem... different," Ingrid commented one afternoon as they reviewed routine reports.

"Different how?" Erik asked, looking up.

"Lighter," Ingrid said with a small smile. "Like you're finally letting yourself exhale."

Erik chuckled. "Maybe I am. Took long enough."

One evening, Erik was invited to speak at a local event honoring the police force. It was held in the town hall, a cozy space filled with familiar faces. As he stood at the podium, looking out at the crowd, he felt an unusual sense of gratitude—not for the recognition, but for the chance to reflect on what they had accomplished together.

"This town has always been a place of resilience," Erik began, his voice steady. "And this team, this community, has shown me the power of standing together, even when the odds feel impossible. Thank you—for trusting us, for believing in us, and for reminding me why I do this job."

The applause was warm and genuine, and as Erik stepped down, Lars clapped him on the back. "Look at you, getting all sentimental," Lars teased.

"Don't get used to it," Erik replied with a smirk.

Ingrid approached Erik after the event, her expression thoughtful. "You know," she began, "I've been thinking about what's next for me."

"Oh?" Erik asked.

"I might take a step back," Ingrid said. "Not leave, but... maybe shift my focus. Teach, maybe. Share what I've learned."

Erik nodded. "You'd be great at that. We've all learned so much from you already."

Ingrid smiled. "What about you? Do you ever think about what's next?"

Erik considered her question. "I do. But for the first time, I don't feel like I have to rush toward an answer. I'm okay with just... being here."

As the snow fell heavier and the days grew shorter, Erik found comfort in the simple joys of the season. He spent more time with Lars and Ingrid, sharing meals and stories, forging bonds that had become more like family than colleagues.

One cold evening, as the three of them gathered at Erik's home, Lars raised his glass in a toast.

"To the past," Lars said, his grin wide. "And to whatever comes next."

"To the future," Ingrid added, clinking her glass with theirs.

"To the now," Erik finished, his voice steady and full of meaning.

They drank to the moment, a rare and precious pause in lives often consumed by chaos.

The Inventory List

The quiet of Smögen was shattered one crisp winter morning. Erik was at the station, sipping his first cup of coffee, when Ingrid burst into his office, her face pale and her voice tight.

“We have a problem,” she said, holding a folder with trembling hands.

“What is it?” Erik asked, his instincts immediately kicking in.

“It’s about the ship,” Ingrid said, placing the folder on his desk. “The one we intercepted from Algren’s compound. There’s something we missed.”

Erik opened the folder, his eyes scanning the documents. It was an inventory list, detailing the ship’s contents. As he read, his stomach turned.

“There was more,” Ingrid continued. “A second shipment left the compound just before we arrived. We didn’t catch it because it was routed through multiple shell companies. But now... it’s surfaced.”

“Where?” Erik demanded.

“Rotterdam,” Ingrid replied. “And Erik, the cargo—it’s worse than we thought. It’s not just weapons. It’s advanced bioagents. Something designed for mass disruption.”

Erik felt the blood drain from his face. “How long have we known this?”

“I only pieced it together an hour ago,” Ingrid said. “Interpol just confirmed it. The ship is scheduled to dock tonight.”

Erik stood, his mind racing. “Lars needs to hear this. Get the team ready. We need to act now.”

The urgency of the situation brought a new kind of tension to the station. Lars arrived moments later, his usual humor replaced by grim focus.

“What’s the plan?” he asked.

“We head to Rotterdam,” Erik said. “If we don’t stop that ship before it unloads, this could be catastrophic.”

The team mobilized quickly, their preparations efficient despite the weight of the mission. By nightfall, they were en route to the port city, the chill of winter following them like a shadow.

The docks in Rotterdam were sprawling and chaotic, a maze of shipping containers and towering cranes. Erik’s team worked closely with local authorities to locate the vessel, their movements shrouded in secrecy to avoid alerting the crew.

“There it is,” Ingrid said, pointing to a massive container ship in the distance. Its dark hull loomed ominously against the lights of the harbor.

Erik nodded, signaling for the team to move in. “No mistakes,” he said. “We secure the ship, the crew, and the cargo. This doesn’t leave the dock.”

The operation began smoothly. Erik and Lars led the charge, their team boarding the ship and sweeping through the decks. They encountered resistance—armed crew members who fought fiercely to protect their cargo. Shots rang out in the cold night air, the sound echoing across the harbor.

As they reached the lower decks, Erik’s unease grew. The containers were heavily secured, their markings indicating hazardous materials. Ingrid, monitoring from a command post onshore, relayed instructions through their earpieces.

“Careful, Erik,” she warned. “If those containers are breached, we could be looking at a disaster.”

“Understood,” Erik replied, his focus razor-sharp. It was in the heart of the ship’s cargo hold that they found the truth. One container, marked with biohazard symbols, was already open.

Inside were vials of a pale, viscous liquid stored in temperature-controlled chambers.

Lars cursed under his breath. “This is bigger than we thought.”

Suddenly, Erik’s radio crackled. “We have movement on the dock!” Ingrid’s voice was urgent. “A second group—they’re here to retrieve the cargo!”

Erik’s blood ran cold. “How many?”

“Too many,” Ingrid replied. “You need to get out of there. Now.”

The chaos that unfolded was unlike anything Erik had ever experienced. The second group was heavily armed, and their assault on the ship was coordinated and ruthless. Erik’s team fought valiantly, but they were outnumbered and outgunned.

“Fall back!” Erik shouted, his voice cutting through the gunfire. “Secure what you can and get to the extraction point!”

Lars was at his side, his weapon blazing as they retreated through the labyrinth of containers. “We’re not leaving without that cargo!”

“We don’t have a choice!” Erik snapped, pulling Lars toward the exit.

As they reached the upper deck, an explosion rocked the ship. Erik was thrown to the ground, his vision blurring as the world tilted around him.

When Erik regained consciousness, the ship was ablaze, its cargo lost to the fire and the chaos. Lars was kneeling beside him, blood streaked across his face.

“We need to move!” Lars shouted, pulling Erik to his feet.

But Erik’s gaze was drawn to the dock, where the shadowy figures of the second group were retreating, carrying several containers with them.

"They're getting away," Erik said, his voice hoarse.

"I know," Lars replied. "We'll stop them another day. But not if we die here."

Reluctantly, Erik followed Lars off the ship, the flames consuming it in their wake.

Back in Smögen, the team reconvened, their exhaustion palpable. Ingrid was waiting for them, her expression a mix of relief and despair.

"The ship..." Erik began, his voice hollow.

"It's all over the news," Ingrid said. "They're calling it an accident, but we know the truth. And those containers—they're still out there."

Erik sat heavily in his chair, his mind racing. The victory they had fought so hard for now felt fragile, incomplete.

"What's our next move?" Lars asked quietly.

Erik's gaze was distant, but his resolve was unshaken. "We find them," he said. "No matter how long it takes."

Printed in Great Britain
by Amazon

60427217R00070